# What the press says about Harlequin Romances…

"…clean, wholesome fiction…always with an upbeat, happy ending."
— *San Francisco Chronicle*

"…a work of art."
— *The Globe & Mail*, Toronto

"Nothing quite like it has happened since *Gone With the Wind*…"
— *Los Angeles Times*

"…among the top ten…"
— *International Herald-Tribune*, Paris

"Women have come to trust these clean, easy-to-read love stories about contemporary people, set in exciting foreign places."
— *Best Sellers*, New York

# OTHER
## *Harlequin Romances*
## by MARY WIBBERLEY

Many of these titles are available at your local bookseller
or through the Harlequin Reader Service.

For a free catalogue listing all available Harlequin Romances,
send your name and address to:

HARLEQUIN READER SERVICE,
M.P.O. Box 707, Niagara Falls, N.Y.  14302
Canadian address: Stratford, Ontario, Canada  N5A 6W2

or use order coupon at back of book.

# Lord of
# the Island

by

## MARY WIBBERLEY

## Harlequin Books

TORONTO • LONDON • NEW YORK • AMSTERDAM • SYDNEY

Original hardcover edition published in 1978
by Mills & Boon Limited

ISBN 0-373-02177-1

Harlequin edition published July 1978

PRINTED IN U.S.A.

# CHAPTER ONE

HE was big, lean, and dangerous—Sally Herrick knew that instinctively the first time she set eyes on him. But she didn't know who he was—not then. She didn't find out for several days, by which time it was too late.

She saw him watching her when she waited for her ticket at the counter, saw his eyes following her as she walked away, and knew with a certain annoyance that when he went afterwards to the same counter and spoke to the airline girl, he was talking about her. She lifted her chin, walked decisively out to the waiting plane, and resisted the temptation to look back. As if I care! she thought. After all that's happened, one staring man isn't going to bother me. She went aboard the baking hot plane, scarcely a degree cooler inside than out, and waited for the take-off. In two hours she would be at Uncle Alistair's. There she would rest, and sunbathe, and let the inner wounds heal, and when she went back to London in six weeks, Simon Raines, her fiancé—her *ex*-fiancé—would be forgotten.

She caught her breath at that thought. Would it be that easy? It's got to be, she told herself fiercely. No one jilts Sally Herrick and gets away with it. He'll pay, one way or another. He'll find out what it's like to be squeezed out of the charmed circle—while I'll still be there in the centre of it, and I'll be tanned and beautiful, and I'll make sure everyone knows I went to my uncle's island for a holiday because London bored me terribly—and the implications will be there, very subtly—that Simon bored me too, and everyone will look at him, and feel sorry for *him*, not me.

She smiled a little half-smile to herself. Sally Herrick, known as the heartbreaker—although she wasn't supposed to be aware of that tag—leader of the small section of London society that went to all the right places at the right times, and weekended in the country at the right houses, was used to having her own way in everything. She had been brought up to expect the best in life, and got it. She stroked her smooth auburn hair reflectively. So far the journey had been comfortable and uneventful, and that was as it should be. And Uncle Alistair would be there to meet her with the Rolls, and would whisk her away to his villa in the hills of Adelana, and there she would meet her aunt Rosa, his second wife. Sally's mouth tightened. She wasn't prepared to like Rosa. Uncle Alistair had always been so easy to twist round her little finger; a woman at the villa was a different proposition. Despite Alistair's glowing descriptions of the new aunt, and the new lease of life she had given him, Sally would have preferred him as she had always known him, the laughing, middle-aged uncle who showered her with presents, and gave her all his attention on his infrequent visits to London. Still, she reflected, I can't have everything. He had invited her there so many times, and there had been no hesitation when she had cabled could she go and visit for a few weeks. The reply had been instant. 'Yes. Come now.'

When was the plane going to move? She looked at the diamond-encrusted Omega on her wrist in annoyance. The hand moved imperceptibly on. Ten past three, and they should have taken off at three. Four other people sat in the plane, a couple, and a woman with a sleeping child in her arms. The man and woman spoke quietly, somewhere outside a tractor started up, and all else was silence. Sally lay back and closed her eyes. She'd give them five minutes, and then she'd be off back to that counter to play hell with somebody . . .

A door slammed, and she looked up. Two people had just come aboard, a small scruffy-looking steward —and the man. The small scruffy steward gave everyone a beaming smile and vanished into the cockpit, and she thought: My God, that's the pilot! And the man, the big, lean, dangerous-looking man, glanced briefly across at her, dismissed her with a look, and sat down in the vacant seat at the opposite side slightly in front.

There was a crackle of static, then the pilot's voice. 'Okay, we're off in a moment. Please fasten your seat-belts.' Silence, then the roar of the engines, and the plane shuddered and trembled, and began to move forward. Sally fought to control her sheer horror at the casualness of it all—as though it was a *bus*—and fastened her seat-belt. The man took a small notebook out of the pocket of his denim jeans and began to read what was written in it. She couldn't help it. She watched him. She told herself it was because there was nothing else to do, and because she was terrified that the rattling crate she found herself in might disintegrate at any second, and it was to take her mind off the sheer awfulness of the idea, but in actual fact, there was something almost compelling about the still figure in that opposite seat. She could see him only in profile, yet that was enough. That he was tall she had already seen, in the waiting hall; but there she hadn't noticed the powerful build of him, the strong head, thick neck and muscular shoulders and arms, bare in the sleeveless denim jacket he wore that stretched tautly over his frame. His hair was short, bleached by the sun—yet his eyebrows, and the glimpse of thick hair at his neck, were dark, as were the hairs covering those tanned and very muscular forearms. He had a stubborn chin, a wide mouth and straight nose—and suddenly, as if aware of her scrutiny, he looked round, and she saw that his eyes were startlingly blue. Yet he looked past her, as if she were scarcely worth a glance, and then back to his notebook.

Sally sensed it again. He was dangerous. She didn't know how she knew, she just *did*. And with that realisation came a second one. He was going to the same place, to the same small island where Uncle Alistair had lorded it for so long—so why hadn't her uncle ever mentioned *him*? Obviously because he was merely a visitor. Sally dismissed the man—with difficulty—from her mind, closed her eyes, and began to plan what she would tell her uncle when she arrived. It couldn't be the simple truth, of course; no, she would imply the same that she had to all her many friends, that London had temporarily lost its appeal, she was bored with the dull April weather, she needed a change, and above all, she wanted to see her favourite uncle again. The last, at least, was true; Alistair Herrick had always had a special place in Sally's affections. She sighed very slightly. That was that, then. Everything cut and dried in her mind, and already the image of Simon beginning to recede. In fact, she was beginning to wonder if she had imagined herself in love with him, simply because it seemed the fashionable thing to do. And she realised the simple fact quite suddenly. It was her pride that had been hurt, not her heart. That was as intact as it always had been, always would be ...

She was surprised to find that she had been asleep, when the cry of the child awoke her. They were coming in to land, and the mother had been gathering several pieces of hand luggage together. Sally blinked a few times, marvelling that she could have slept through the rattling and juddering which seemed to be getting rapidly worse as they lost height. She looked out of the porthole to see lush green trees below, the roofs of houses, and nearer, a sandy beach, the sand nearly pure white like salt, and the water lapping it a deep green. She sighed a sigh of contentment. This would do quite nicely, until she was ready for London again. She opened her handbag to check her passport and wallet were safe, then looked up. The man was watching her. He had turned his head, it was no accidental glance. The usual thing was to look away, it was an unwritten rule—only he had clearly never heard of that one. He not only didn't look away, he remained staring at her as if trying to memorise her features. And Sally, to her own chagrin, found that she was the one who had to drop her eyes. A prickle of resentment coloured her face. The arrogance of the man! There was nothing remotely admiring in that very personal glance—she was used to that, and had learned the dismissive look that effectively brushed off any attempt at picking up from strange men—it was more an unsubtle weighing up that she found suddenly disturbing. Damn him, she thought. First at the airstrip, now here. Who the hell does he think he is? She took a deep breath and looked sharply up, prepared to wither him with one blast of her green eyes, only now he was talking to the woman with the child, and she felt very foolish.

Five minutes later, as the plane taxied to a halt, she forgot the aggressive fellow passenger as she peered out at the primitive landing strip, huts in the background, a few cars parked, glittering in the sunlight, and a cluster of people waiting. She lifted her hand, seeing her uncle, seeing the small dark-haired woman by his side—her mouth tightened. They were holding hands! Now that was ridiculous, almost embarrassing. Didn't they realise how foolish they must look—a man of fifty-five, and the woman by his side barely thirty—and holding hands like a couple of teenage hippies? Sally forced herself to breathe calmly and deeply. First that *man*, now this—her mood of cool confidence, of being in control of everything, was rapidly disintegrating, and it didn't suit her at all. She had only minutes to regain her self-possession, and she must do it, she must.

There was a grinding crackling as if the undercarriage had just crumpled like tissue paper, and then silence, calm, stillness. They had actually made it! Sally gathered her handbag and make-up case together, and waited for the other passengers to leave before her. She sat and watched their preparations for departure, sat and calmly watched as the tall man helped the woman with her bags, heard him laugh at something she said, saw the man with the woman turn and also say something, watched them all leave the plane—except the tall man, who vanished into the cockpit.

It was time to go. If she sat there any longer *he* might think she was waiting for him. Sally rose smoothly and walked down the primitive wooden staircase and into her uncle's waiting arms. The heat blast nearly knocked her off her feet and she gasped at that, and the sheer exuberance of her uncle's embrace.

'Lovely to see you, my dear Sally,' he said, kissing her warmly on both cheeks, 'and this is your aunt Rosa.' He drew the smaller woman into the circle of his embrace, and she and Sally looked at one another, the age-old, instinctive sizing up being made even as they smiled and murmured the conventional greetings. Small, dark and young—scarcely five years older than Sally herself—Rosa might be, but Sally realised with almost a sense of shock that this was no ordinary woman. Her clear eyes met Sally's with that certain look that said everything in one glance. 'You don't frighten me, honey.' Permanently unspoken, the words would never—*could* never—be said, but they were there all the same, and on record, and Sally suddenly knew that her days as Uncle Alistair's number one favourite were over.

'Right then, off we go, back to the house—bet you could do with a cool shower, eh, Sal?' Alistair chuckled, taking her arm. Somewhere in the distance behind them, a youth trundled along with Sally's cases on a trolley, and she glanced back to see the plane shimmering in the heat, but no one visible. She turned away. If Rosa hadn't been there, walking and talking and laughing the other side of Alistair, Sally would have made a joke about the man, and described him—casually, of course—but Rosa's presence inhibited that. It didn't matter. He was probably a visitor to the island, although why should he go and talk to the pilot if so—'Sorry?'

'You're miles away! I said—here we are, in you get!'

But there was no Rolls—at least, not where they stood. Just a rather battered old Morris whose paintwork had seen better days. Sally swallowed. She wondered, just for a moment, if she was asleep on the plane, and in the middle of a dream.

Alistair had always been of a shrewd mind. He laughed. 'Sorry, love, the Rolls has gone. This is more economical, so here we go with your cases—thanks, Tommy,' this to the native boy who had at last caught them up with the trolley and was busily unloading Sally's luggage. In the mild confusion, Sally looked around her at the now distant huts and plane, and the few people. Everything had an unreal, dreamlike quality to it, the brilliance of the light lending colour and force to the surroundings, and the people moved, and a bird swooped and wheeled in the air, and Sally thought, everything is subtly different from what I expected, and Uncle Alistair is changed too, and it's all slightly wrong and I don't know why, and I'm disturbed by it all . . .

But there was no time, and it was too late, they were getting in the car and the heat was unbearable, and for a second, just a split second, Sally caught Rosa's eyes, and she saw in them a distinct warning. Her supreme self-confidence wavered momentarily, then reasserted itself. I'm here on holiday, she told herself as they rattled away from the airstrip, and I will enjoy myself. But there were more surprises to come.

The bungalow was long, red-roofed and modest. Cleanly white and sparkling, with colourful flowers growing in profusion around it, it had a cheerful atmosphere—but it was by no means a villa, and it wasn't remotely like the photographs Sally had once seen of her uncle's previous home.

'We moved,' he said cheerfully as he lifted out Sally's cases from the boot, 'and we never got round to telling you, did we, Rosa love?' He laughed, and they all went in to the cool hallway.

'I'll show you your bedroom,' said Rosa calmly. 'Leave the cases there, Alistair, I'll be back in a minute. Come on, Sally.'

The two women walked down a corridor to a room at the end, and Rosa flung open a door to reveal a small neat pleasant room, prettily furnished. As Sally went in she heard the door click shut behind her, and turned to see Rosa standing by it.

She spoke quietly, but her words were clear enough. 'You're puzzled, aren't you?' she said. There was a small smile about her mouth, but her eyes were cool and hard as she looked at Sally.

Sally returned the glance with one of equal hardness and for a moment their eyes met in a silent clash. The summing up, the one begun at the airstrip, was now complete. And Sally knew she had met a woman who would never be intimidated by her.

'Yes, I am,' she admitted. 'It's all—so different,' she shrugged.

'It is,' Rosa nodded. 'You're right. The villa's gone, the Rolls has gone—but you noticed that ages ago, didn't you? And we live on very little money—*my* money—and I dare say I'll tell you about it later, but just for now I'll tell you something else. Your uncle isn't well, in fact he's a very sick man, but he doesn't know it, and if it had been left to me I wouldn't have had you here because I know all about you and I don't like what I know, but Alistair is my husband and I love him very much, and if it makes *him* happy to see you then that's fine by me!' She paused, presumably for breath, and Sally didn't say a word because she was hearing things the like of which she had never heard before from anyone, and she was too stunned to speak.

'I'm not sure if you can understand what I'm saying,' Rosa went on, 'so I'll put it to you simply. If you upset him in any way, you'll be out of here so fast your feet won't touch the ground.' She smiled again.

'I know you came here prepared not to like me—I'd "stolen" your favourite uncle, hadn't I? But you know nothing—you think you can step out from your London society friends when it suits you ...'

Sally went to sit on the bed, because for some strange reason her legs had gone weak. Rosa paused until she was sitting, then went on: 'I've got friends in London too. Does that surprise you? It shouldn't —and I know all about the life you lead. I know much more about you than you think, but I hadn't met you before—now I have, and you're just like I expected.'

There was a small silence, then Sally found her voice. 'You've made yourself perfectly clear,' she said. 'And you're right, I came here intending to dislike you.' She looked up at her aunt, and something on Sally's face made the older woman's eyes narrow. 'But you're wrong about one thing. I would never do anything to upset Uncle Alistair. You say he's sick— I didn't know that. What what is wrong?'

Rosa's face softened. 'I don't want to talk about it —yet. I may do later, when he's gone to bed. He has to go at nine every night, you know—no, you didn't know, did you? How could you?'

Sally put her hand to her face. She was more shattered than she could ever have imagined she would be. Nothing like this had ever happened to her before. It was as if her whole world shifted, like a quicksand, and nothing was safe any more. Rosa's voice, when she spoke again, was more gentle.

'I've been hard on you,' she said. 'I did it deliberately because——' She stopped, and Sally looked up.

'Yes? Because?' she said.

'Because—I was frightened of you——'

Sally's laugh was shaky. 'Frightened—of me? My God, you've just *terrified* me!'

Then suddenly the tension eased. Inexplicably, regarding the circumstances, but it was so. Rosa walked over to the bed and stood in front of her. 'Yes, I had to. You see, I knew the power you wield—yet my feelings for Alistair are so much stronger that it didn't matter. Nothing matters except him. Does that sound odd to you? I'm his second wife, twenty-five years younger than him, and he will never be hurt by anyone while I'm around, and I thought you would, and I dreaded your coming because of who you are— only now I see you clearly, and I'm not frightened of you.' She paused, and in that infinitesimal silence Sally knew with dread certainty, what was to come. 'I'm sorry for you.'

The words hung in the air, and it seemed that they softly echoed round the room. Sally stood up. She was taller than Rosa. 'You don't need to be,' she whispered fiercely. 'Why did you say that?'

Rosa smiled. 'I think you already know, inside yourself.' She partly turned away and went to a door in the corner of the room and flung it open. 'There's your shower. While you're in there, I'll bring your cases along. Dinner will be ready in half an hour.' Then she walked out, leaving Sally alone.

For a few moments Sally didn't move, then she crossed over to the shower room, went in and closed the door behind her. She thought nothing could ever be worse than what had just happened, and she needed time alone to think. But it had only just begun.

The following morning Sally walked down to the village on her own to send a cable to her mother telling her of her safe arrival. The events of the previous evening were still etched with startling clarity in her mind, the scene in her room more clear than what had happened afterwards when she and Rosa had been alone talking after Uncle Alistair had gone to bed. Yet what Rosa had had to say then was more important than what had gone before. She had told Sally that Uncle Alistair hadn't got long to live. Six months—a year, that was all. He knew nothing of this, thought only that he had a mild blood disorder that necessitated rest and good food. And his money had been gambled away years before. That came as no surprise to Sally, who had always known him as a heavy gambler in her younger days, when, then, his luck had always been in. It was the illness that had stunned her, the knowledge that he was dying, and that nothing could be done about it. Rosa had made her promise not to tell anyone, not even her mother, Alistair's sister-in-law, and Sally had given her word.

After the talk, when she had gone to bed, she had thought over Rosa's words, and the image of her face had come into Sally's mind, and her last waking thought, before she fell into a deep, troubled sleep, had been: Rosa is a far stronger and better woman than I could ever be. When she had woken in the morning, the taste of tears had been on her lips, and the sting of them in her eyes, and her own safe, secure little world hadn't seemed quite so wonderful after all.

She began to think her imagination was working overtime. Yet there was something almost tangible in the way the villagers spoke to her and looked at her—as if they knew something that she didn't. As if they shared some secret in which she could have no part—and yet which was in a way about her. It made her oddly uneasy, and she went to sit on a bench at the quayside in the shade of a tall palm tree to think about it. There was nothing she could put a finger on, and yet ...

'You are here on holiday?' the woman at the post office had enquired, soft-eyed, smiling. 'It is beautiful here, yes?'

'Yes, indeed,' Sally had agreed.

'You must go a visit to Isle of Dreams,' the little postmistress had added, rolling her eyes. 'Is beautiful —is good for visitors.'

'I'll remember that.' Sally had gone out, had heard the whispered voices as the woman turned to someone standing in the shadows at the back of the shop. Then, later, as she had sat drinking an iced lemonade outside the beach café, the young native waiter had brought her a second drink 'on the house', and had paused to say : 'Ah, you visit the island soon, eh, while you are here?'

'The island?'

'Island of Dreams—ah!' he had waved his hands expressively. 'You must go there—so beautiful.'

'Yes, I must.' She thought, cynically, and I wonder

how much that will cost me? Perhaps they got commission for everyone they persuaded to go. But a bigger surprise came when she walked back to the bungalow, and mentioned it to Rosa. They were in the kitchen, Uncle Alistair sat outside in the shade, and Rosa prepared a salad lunch. She whirled round on Sally at the mention of the island.

'*That* place!' Her eyes went cold. 'Don't mention it to Alistair.'

'Why not?' Sally felt the force of Rosa's reaction.

'Because the man who owns it is called Luke Vilis — and if it wasn't for him Alistair would still have his villa and his money——'

'You mean he robbed Uncle——'

'Robbed? if you like. The man's a ruthless bas——' she checked herself visibly. 'Just don't mention his name here.'

'All right, I won't. Does this Luke—this man *live* on the island?'

'He stays there occasionally, yes. And on this place, and he travels all over the world. And if I don't see him ever again, it will be too soon. I could kill him.' She looked at Sally, and her eyes were bright with unshed tears. 'I would rather you didn't go there—at all.'

# CHAPTER TWO

But that had been the wrong thing to say to Sally. It was a challenge—and no one ever told her what to do, especially not Rosa. The civilised veneer was thin. Both were pleasant to each other in Alistair's presence, but the deep down instinctive feelings were there all the time, and later that day, as Sally finished her unpacking, a small well of excitement bubbled inside her. If Uncle Alistair hated this man Luke Vilis, then she did too. But she would not be forbidden, like a child, from going to the island that he owned. No one need even know. It had been made clear by Rosa that Sally would be left to her own devices, that she was to come and go as she pleased, within reason, and that if she wished to stay out sunbathing or swimming for the entire day, that would be fine by them both.

She went over to the window and looked out at the gently sloping gardens leading to the sea. In the distance a smudgy blue blur of land—the Island of Dreams—lay in the water. What a ridiculous name, Sally thought, like something out of a film, a mushy romance. And it was owned by a man with a foreign-sounding name, who had either won Uncle Alistair's money from him—or stolen it. Rosa had refused to be more specific. It was as if, after her first impassioned outburst, she had wanted to change the subject. She had done so, despite Sally's attempts to learn more, and had then called Alistair in, thus effectively closing the matter. But Sally remained intrigued. She didn't even want to meet the man, just to *see* his island. Her mental picture of him was unattractive enough, a swarthy, middle-aged individual, probably balding, and almost certainly with a droopy moustache ... She shivered. 'I would rather you didn't go there,' Rosa had said. And Rosa didn't like Sally. But then Rosa would never know, and certainly Uncle Alistair wouldn't—but Sally was going to the island just for a short visit. Just to see, and *know* she had been.

Once the idea had been thought of, it was as good as done, for Sally always did exactly as she wanted, and always would do. She began to plan it very carefully.

She would be out for the day, she told them next morning at breakfast, and would it be all right if she took a few sandwiches and a flask with her? She was going to find a quiet stretch of beach to sunbathe and swim. The lies came easily, and she hugged her uncle warmly when he made mild protest and said, but wouldn't it be dull for her?

'I'm going to go home with the best tan *ever*,' she had laughed. 'I'll be the envy of all my friends,' and she had seen Rosa's half smile, but it hadn't mattered. She didn't really care what Rosa thought about her any more, for her own natural confidence had reasserted itself, and blanked out that unfortunate remark of the other woman's about feeling sorry for Sally, so that it might never have been said.

She set off about eleven, and walked slowly to the

village to where the boats bobbed in the harbour. A cruise liner was in, and tourists jostled in the busy market place, buying their souvenirs to take home to Seattle or Southampton, and Sally thought, there'll probably be a boat trip going anyway. But there wasn't, when she asked, so that eventually she found her way to the beachside café and sat down. It was busy, several brightly clad day trippers from the boat sitting there sipping their aperitifs and drinking in the local colour at the same time. Busy—but not so much so that her little waiter couldn't find time to come over and talk. Almost as if, she reflected later, he had been expecting her.

'Can I get a boat to take me to the Island?' she asked. She didn't believe in wasting words, or time, once her mind was made up.

He looked thoughtful. 'Ah, you wish to go? Good. You will like—but alas, everyone is busy today—these tourists, you know.' He grinned, showing a mouthful of strong white teeth. 'But I do know someone——' He hesitated. To be thwarted was not in Sally's book.

'I'll pay,' she said, adding sweetly, 'well.'

'One moment, please.' He darted away, vanished inside the café, to return a few minutes later with a tray of drinks, and Sally's Coca-Cola. 'Now, enough ice, yes? Okay. Oh yes, a—someone will maybe take you.' He pointed further along to where a white-painted boat bobbed at the jetty. 'See there, the boat called *Astrid*?'

'Yes,' Sally nodded.

'You go there, five minutes maybe, ask Lucky to take you.'

'Lucky? That's a name?'

'Yes,' he grinned. 'Okay. S'cuse, I must go,' and he darted away. Sally sipped her drink and surveyed the motley throng of tourists. What a dull crowd they were, despite the jazzy clothes. Middle-aged couples, giggling like teenagers, the women with blue-rinsed hair and huge sunglasses, the men balding and paunchy . . . She felt suddenly bored with everything, bored and disgusted. She wouldn't have been here if it hadn't been for Simon. She looked down at the sparkling drink, the ice cubes melting rapidly. He'd be sorry for what he'd done! Just because there had been that scene in the restaurant—and then dropping her off at her flat and telling her she was the most selfish, spoilt bitch he'd ever met in his life. Sally gripped the glass so hard that her knuckles showed white. They'd had the mother and father of a row there in the street, and he'd driven off, brakes squealing, his final words echoing in her ears. 'That's it—we're through. I'm off to Oslo in the morning and I don't know when I'll be back.'

Just like that, he had gone. And Sally, knowing that the best form of defence is attack—at least in her circle—had made a few phone calls, made sure everyone knew that Simon now bored her, and that she was going away for a holiday, had sent the cable to Uncle Alistair, packed up and left London. If Alistair hadn't been able to put her up, she would have gone abroad somewhere else, anywhere, because the ploy was not to be left behind. And now she was here, on a remote island in the Indian Ocean, and it would appear to everyone that poor Simon had been jilted. Poor Simon!

She left a tip by the glass and set off without a backward glance at the curious tourists who, she knew, would be staring at the tall, beautiful redhead and wondering who she was. She was quite used to that, well used to admiring stares. The man on the plane, the one who had stared at her in a most disconcerting and decidedly unadmiring way, she had practically forgotten about, so that it was rather odd that she should think of him a moment later as she strolled along the white sand. She wondered fleetingly where he was, who he was—and if she would ever see him again.

The boat rocked slightly as she stepped aboard, and she called out:

'Anybody home?'

A voice floated up from the cabin. 'Yes, you want something?' It was a deep brown voice, decidedly attractive.

She bent down, but the cabin was shadowy after the sun. 'Are you Lucky?' she asked. There were several steps, and she could see nothing.

A rich laugh. 'Sometimes. Why?'

That's all I need, a comedian, she thought. 'I want to go to the Island,' she said coolly. 'I was told Lucky would take me—may I come down, or are you coming up?'

'Come down. I'm busy—I don't bite, you're quite safe.'

'I didn't imagine you did—oh!' She was standing in the doorway of the small cabin, and the man with his back to her was just straightening up, turning—and she saw his face, and shadowed though it was, she recognised him. There was an instant of shocked surprise, then she spoke again. 'I'm sorry, I must have got the wrong boat.'

If he had stared at her before on the plane, that was nothing compared to the way he looked at her now. Cool, dark, assessing, and she saw him full face properly for the first time, and the strength and the sense of danger was there too; then he smiled, and the features were transformed.

'No, you haven't got the wrong boat, and yes, some call me "Lucky", and I'll take you now.'

'But I——' she hesitated. What did you say? I find you frightening and I want to go, but not with you.

'It won't cost you a lot. I'm ready now,' he said, and looked at her, and it was as if he read her mind, as if, somehow, he *knew*.

'Can I—can we book it for tomorrow?' she asked.

'No.' He looked at his watch. 'It's only a half-hour run. Wait there.' He walked towards her, and for a moment, blind panic filled her so that she wanted to scream and run—then he had moved past her, and the boat rocked ever so slightly, and Sally was afraid, suddenly so afraid that she reached out her hand and touched his arm. She felt the whipcord muscular strength under her fingers just in that instant before she took her hand away.

'Wait—I've changed my mind,' she said. Her voice had gone faint so that the words came out as a whisper. He stopped, turned, and he was in the doorway of the cabin so that she couldn't get past him if she wanted to.

'I don't understand,' he said slowly. 'You come along to hire my boat to take you to the Island—*you* ask *me*—and now, suddenly, you no longer want to go. Do I frighten you or something?'

'Of—of course not.' She cleared her throat.

'Have you remembered an urgent appointment elsewhere, maybe?' The mockery was subtly challenging in itself. His mouth was wide, lips curving in a half smile, the eyes softening slightly. He shrugged and held his hands out. 'Would you prefer a chaperone? Your aunt Rosa, perhaps?'

'You know who I am?'

'Of course.' He smiled gently, and his face was no longer that hard frightening one she had seen so clearly before. He looked amused, pleasant, diffident. 'I know your uncle too.'

Sally relaxed slightly. She had just made herself look an absolute and utter fool. She wasn't in a strange alien place, and this was no stranger. Just because he had looked at her in a certain way on the plane—she had been nervy then, it had all been her imagination. The important thing now was to erase any wrong impressions she had created in his mind. She laughed. 'You'll think me very stupid,' she said, 'only it's just —well, a rather silly thing. You see, I'd planned to sunbathe today, and I changed my mind, and when I got here, I thought—oh, perhaps I should have let them know, in case they'd wanted to come as well, you see——' The explanation sounded rather feeble to her own ears, but he appeared to be accepting it quite naturally. He laughed.

'Of course! Not to worry. *I* won't say anything. Then, if they do want to go some time you don't have to let them know you've already been, do you?' And he gave her the most beautiful smile, turned, and ran up the steps. Sally stood there thinking about his words, and heard the engines roar into life.

As she went up on to the deck, her fears returned. But then it was too late, for he had cast off and the boat was already swinging out to sea. She looked back at the rapidly receding shoreline, and it seemed to her that she saw the young waiter waving to her from the café, but it might have been her imagination. The man turned round from his place at the wheel and looked at her, then began to laugh.

She stared helplessly at him. His laughter was not like that of before. It was different—and he was different too. And she suddenly knew, in a wave of icy awareness, that her very first impression of him, when she had seen him at the airport, had been the right one. In a way she did not yet understand, but in a way that made all her warning instincts cry out, she knew he was a dangerous man to know. But she still didn't know *who* he was.

She waited by the cabin, holding on to a rail, and watched him steering the boat out from Adelana Island towards the other, ridiculously named Island of Dreams, and her thoughts were chaotic. She began to assemble them into some sort of order. She had taken a dislike to him the first time she had seen him, and then found him looking hard at her. And this morning, a friendly young waiter had told her that his name was Lucky and he would possibly be able to take her to a certain island, a mere half hour trip by sea, and as it was a place neither her uncle nor his wife would want her to go, she was, not unnaturally, a shade nervous about it. That was all—it was quite logical. Only it wasn't all. There was something more, but she couldn't put her finger on it, and . . .

'A drink?' he called from the wheel without looking round. 'Want a drink?'

It *was* her imagination. He was perfectly civil. He had just offered her a drink, and he wasn't laughing, and there was nothing sinister about his face at all. Sally decided it was time she pulled herself together. She'd hired him, after all. She'd be paying for the drink anyway. 'Yes, please. Shall I get it?'

'Yes. Fridge in the galley. Help yourself—and bring me up a Coke with ice in, please.'

She went down slowly, found the galley and the small refrigerator, and poured two Cokes, adding plenty of ice to each glass before carrying them carefully up the steps and on to the deck.

'Thanks.' He took his without looking round. 'Sit down somewhere, make yourself comfortable. We'll be there in about fifteen minutes.' He began to whistle softly as he handed her back the empty glass. But he wasn't looking at her. He was concentrating on what he was doing, keeping the boat on a steady course towards the island which grew rapidly nearer while Adelana receded into the hazy blue distance. Sally looked at him, watched his back as he stood there, and there was a tautness about him, a tension that was not only concentration, it was more. It was—but she couldn't decide what it was, only that the uneasy feeling was back again, and there was nothing she could do about it.

I'm either stupid—or I'm going mad, she thought, and either way if I allow my thoughts to get out of control like this, it's going to spoil my day, so—she took a deep breath, turned away deliberately from the man she only knew as Lucky, and looked out to sea, turning her face to the sun, closing her eyes, making her mind a pleasant blank. It wasn't easy, but her own iron will eventually overcame all her previous doubts, so that when he shouted: 'Nearly there, hold tight, I'm going to swing round,' she was able to reply:

'Fine.'

She watched him manoeuvre the boat in, and it clug-clugged to a slow gentle movement, then he flung out a rope, looped it expertly round a stone stanchion, and moored the vessel by the wooden jetty.

Then silence. And with it Sally realised that for some reason she had expected to see people, and houses, but there was nothing save a fabulous stretch of white sand, trees, and water.

He helped her on to the jetty. 'What now?' he asked.

'I'd like to explore the island,' she answered. 'Will you wait, or come back for me later?'

He gave her an odd look. 'I'm staying,' he said.

'Are there—er—many other people here? Only I don't see——'

'Only us.' He looked down at her as she stood facing him on that wooden jetty, and smiled at her.

And now—and now she saw him properly, really properly, close up for the first time, and there was no more imagining, or doubt, or wondering about anything. Now she knew, and she was more frightened than she had ever been in her life before. The darkly tanned handsome face looked down at her, the smile about his wide mouth, the laughter lines at his eyes, the sun-bleached hair, the strength that lay all about him, the sheer physical magnificence of him, all crystallised in that one smile that said so much—and yet told her nothing save that she was here completely alone with him. And that was enough.

'Who are you?' she whispered.

The startling blue eyes narrowed. 'Don't you *know*?'

'Only that you're called Lucky.' She wanted to run away, but where could she go?

'Lucky—yes. That's the way they say my name. It's a derivation of Luke.'

She closed her eyes. Oh God, she thought, I think I've known all along. 'Luke—Vilis?'

'Yes.'

'I want to go back—now.'

'We're not going back. We're staying here.'

'But—I don't understand. Why . . .?'

'You will.' He turned away from her. 'Come with me.'

'I'm staying here,' she answered defiantly. 'I'm not going anywhere with you—I'm going back to Adelana——'

'Not until I'm ready to take you, and that won't be

for a while. And if you don't walk with me now I shall pick you up and carry you. You can scream as loudly as you like, there's no one to hear. There's just you and me on this island.' He turned back to face her. 'Do you understand me? I mean exactly what I say.'

'You're mad!' she gasped.

The grin broadened. 'Possibly. You'll have to humour me then, won't you?'

'How can I when I don't know why?' she snapped. 'You bring me here and then start talking in this outrageous manner——' She looked around for anything that she could be used as a weapon. She carried only her beach bag. The holdall with her flask and sandwiches was still in the cabin. If she could get to that—there was an aerosol can of sun tan lotion—she turned and jumped on board the boat, and he, swift as thought, was after her, holding her arm, turning her to face him—

'Let me go!' She pushed him violently, and the boat rocked, and he laughed, unmoving, and merely pulled her closer to him.

'Let you go? Are you going to make me? Try, then.' His fingers on her arm were like steel, and Sally scratched at them with her free hand, but to no avail. He merely took that hand as well, and held it. 'You see,' he said softly, 'you haven't a cat in hell's chance of getting free of me. And how do you like that, eh?'

She allowed herself to relax her body slightly. Physically she was no match for him, and she knew it. She might just have to do as he suggested, and humour him. 'All right, I'm not going to struggle. You can let me go,' she said quietly, and he did so. 'But at least you might tell me why you've brought me here.'

'I thought I might save that moment until later,' he answered. 'So you'll just have to be patient.' He smiled—only it wasn't a pleasant smile, it was in a way far worse than the cold scrutiny on the plane. Sally began to shiver helplessly, despite the intense heat. She was remembering the way in which people had told her about this place—the knowing smiles that she had decided she must have been imagining, the feeling that they all knew something she didn't. And now . . .

'You arranged this, didn't you?' she accused. 'You somehow got people to make me want to come here—it wasn't by chance *you* were the only one who had a boat ready. Did that little waiter phone you or something?'

His eyes narrowed. 'You're brighter than I thought. Well, well, there's a surprise. You're quite right, I made up my mind as soon as I saw you that one way or another, I'd get you here—and now I have. I always do what I want.'

'It's because—because of Uncle Alistair, isn't it?' she asked.

The answer surprised her. 'No. Why should it have anything to do with him?'

'Because he hates you—because you robbed him——'

His laughter cut her off in mid-sentence. 'Is that what he told you? Or was it Rosa who said that?'

It was getting worse. All the time, this feeling, this *awful* feeling of being on the fringes of something terrible was growing inside Sally, and she had the sensation of utter helplessness.

She shook her head. 'Never mind, I——' She stopped. Tears weren't far away.

He gripped her arm. 'Don't stop there. Finish what you were going to say. Are you afraid of me?'

She met his eyes defiantly. 'What am I supposed to answer to that? No, I'm enjoying every minute? How would you feel if someone practically kidnapped you and then wouldn't say why?' The fire was back in her eyes. She wasn't beaten yet. She still didn't know what was happening, but she was a fighter. The tears glistened in her eyes and she blinked them away. She wouldn't show any weakness in front of him.

He nodded. 'You've a point. I'd react like you—probably. That is, if I was stupid enough to get myself in such a situation.'

'So I'm stupid now, am I?' Her eyes sparkled. 'Thanks!'

'Yes. Very stupid.' The words hung in the air, and he added softly: 'I've waited quite a while for this moment. Now, are you coming up to the house with me under your own steam, or not?'

'House? There's a house? Who ...'

'Mine. And no one there.'

'You must be joking! You think I'd be silly enough to ...'

He didn't bother to interrupt her, he just leaned forward, swept her into his arms and stepped on to the jetty with her kicking and struggling furiously. 'Let me go *at* once! How dare ...'

'*Don't* do *that.*' The grip round her shoulders and

knees tightened imperceptibly, and she winced with pain.

'Ouch! You've hurt ...'

'Then don't fight. I don't like it, and when I don't like something I stop it.' And again she felt the hardness of his muscular arms as they tightened.

'All right,' she gasped. 'I won't—I'll walk. Please— let me walk.'

He dumped her down on the jetty like a sack of potatoes, and caught her hand instead. 'Walk, then.'

She had to nearly run to keep up with him, so fast did he stride along. It was like a nightmare, except that it was no dream, it was real, and it was happening, and—perhaps worst of all—she *didn't know why*. She twisted her ankle when she tripped over a stone, but he didn't slow, even when she began hopping along, gasping:

'Oh! Ouch—slow down, please—my ankle——'

'You'll live,' was the laconic answer, but he slowed his steps slightly, and they crossed the sand, went into the shadowy greenness of trees, where it was slightly cooler, but damp, along and along, for ever and ever, until ...

'No! That's it!' shouted Sally. 'That's *it*! I've had enough, I'm not—I won't——' but her words were lost as he swept her into his arms again, picked her up like he would a baby, and, scarcely having faltered in his stride, walked on. She screamed, she battered at him with her fists, she pummelled his chest and shoulders and face—and he merely tightened his hold as though her blows were no more effective than a child's. Weak, frightened, she began to cry. 'Please,' she gasped through her sobs, 'let me go——'

'No. We're nearly there. Shut up and relax.'

'Relax? How can I when you're holding me——'

'You can. See, there's the house. Nice, here? Not like a prison?'

It was the oddness of his words, as though he meant something else—as though ... 'You're going to keep me here, aren't you?'

'Yes. Oh yes, I am.' He put her down, and she rubbed her waist where his arm had held her tightly, and she looked at the house. Not a prison indeed, but a beautiful villa, but it might well have been, for all its beauty, because *he* had brought her there, and he had a reason—what, she didn't know, but she was soon to find out.

'Now,' he said, 'let's go inside. I'm sure you could do with a drink.' And he indicated with his arm that she was to walk ahead of him. Sally went up the three white steps and he pushed open the door. It was cool inside, shadowy and lovely, and he closed the door softly after them, and said: 'The kitchen's this way. Come.'

She followed, because she had no choice, because even if she ran she wouldn't get away, and because, for the moment, he seemed reasonably sane. And lastly because, despite everything else, she wanted to know why he had brought her there.

'Sit down.' The kitchen was large and airy, with a grey-tiled floor and white fittings. A fan whirred in the ceiling, the refrigerator hummed away quietly in the corner, and he crossed to it and opened it, revealing the well stocked interior, and she knew with a shock of further surprise that the house had been waiting for her arrival. She sat down on a tall stool and waited. Because she knew that soon, very soon, he was going to tell her why he had abducted her.

'Rum? Brandy? Whisky?'

'No. Fruit juice, please.'

He gave her a cool look. 'Keeping sober?'

'Isn't it better I should?'

He didn't answer. He poured out some juice from a jug in the refrigerator, and she took it. She sniffed it, and he said: 'It's not drugged, if that's what you're thinking. It's pure pineapple juice.'

'You don't mind if I don't trust you, do you?'

'I would hardly expect otherwise.' However, he poured some of the juice for himself and drank it. 'See?'

Sally sipped her drink and watched him.

'I don't need drugs to keep you here,' he said, in a matter-of-fact tone. 'You'll stay anyway.'

'Will I? Are you sure?' She was as calm as he now.

'You can't get away. It's as simple as that.' He shrugged and added a generous measure of Bacardi rum to his fruit juice. 'Cheers.' She ignored the salutation, turned away and looked out of the window.

'You'd like to know why I brought you here, wouldn't you?'

'You mean you're going to tell me? Golly!'

He grinned faintly at her sarcasm. 'Yes. Your name's Sally Herrick, you live in London, and you're spoilt, rich, and you always, but always, get your own way. Right?'

'If you say so,' she shrugged.

'I do say so. And you consider that life centres round you, and your little circle of "important" friends, and as long as everything goes smoothly for *you*, regardless of what it's like for other people, then that's that. You're happy.'

She feigned a yawn. 'You bore me.'

'I'll do more than bore you before I've finished.'

She looked at him then. 'Oh, I'm sure you've got lots of little surprises for me. Go ahead. You have a captive audience, haven't you? I'm here, I can't get away, and if you want to insult me, you can. So——' She smiled at him and sipped her drink.

'You're a cool one, you know that? A real cool bitch—and I do mean A1, eighteen carat bitch.' His eyes glinted darkly. 'But by God, you won't have that smile on your face when I've finished with you.' He drank some of his drink. 'Because I'm going to teach you a lesson you won't forget as long as you live. I've waited three years for this moment, and now it's here.' He paused, then added more softly: 'And you still don't know why, do you?'

Three years? What did that mean? He was talking in riddles, awful nightmare riddles that caused her heart to beat faster. 'Until yesterday I'd never heard of you,' she answered, 'so how——'

'No, not of me. But you knew my sister, and you knew her fiancé, and you set out deliberately to steal him from her, and succeeded. Only you didn't care what happened to her afterwards, did you? You'd had your bit of fun—that was all that mattered. She had a nervous breakdown——'

'Stop! I don't know what you're talking about,' she interrupted desperately.

'Then I'll refresh your failing memory. Leonora Jervis—and Julian Kingston——'

The room seemed to grow darker, tilting and beginning to whirl round as Sally clutched the table, dizziness overwhelming her as memory flooded back. Oh God, she thought—I don't believe it—

'I can see you know what I'm talking about. Good. It will give you time to think about it when I'm gone.' He put his empty glass down on the table and left the room. She heard the outer door close, and then silence filled the air. She was alone. She didn't realise how alone until she went out and saw the boat speeding away across the water.

# CHAPTER THREE

SALLY leaned against the door post and watched the small boat growing smaller in the water, saw Adelana Island in the misty distance, and wanted to scream. She put her hands to her head and fought rising panic. She hated being alone, and she was just that, alone on an island, left there by a man who had just told her something overwhelmingly shattering. She sat down on the step because her legs wouldn't support her, and she wrapped her arms around her and rocked herself backwards and forwards in pain.

Now there was not even the distant sound of the boat's engine, just silence. An awful enveloping silence that filled her, surrounded her, overwhelmed her. Then Leonora's face swam into view, the beautiful face of the dark-haired girl who had been invited into Sally's circle, and had brought her fiancé with her, Julian Kingston, tall, dark and devastatingly attractive. Sally had seen him, and wanted him instantly. The men in her circle were becoming boring. This was a new face, and his obvious devotion to Leonora only made him more of a challenge. And Sally always got what she wanted . . .

The only trouble was, as she had realised later, that Julian wasn't all that much fun. He wasn't particularly wealthy, for a start, and while it was always pleasant to have a handsome man in tow, once the novelty of capturing him had worn off, she began to lose interest rapidly. She had made the conquest, had been seen to have made it, that was the important thing—and then it became boring. So she dropped him, and went to visit cousins in America for a holiday, came back refreshed, and resumed the social round. And Julian and Leonora had been forgotten as quickly as that.

What had Luke said? Leonora had had a nervous breakdown? How ridiculous, thought Sally, people don't have nervous breakdowns over something as trivial as a broken engagement, she must have been neurotic to start with ... She shivered, despite the intense heat. She'd go mad if she had to stay here any longer. The feeling of loneliness was oppressive and frightening. She had to get away. She had to, or she would die. She stood up and walked into the house. There might be a telephone. If she could phone for help ...

There was one, in a room off the hall, and she ran to it, heart beating fast, and picked it up. But it was dead. As she put it back she heard a droning noise from outside, growing louder, ran quickly back into the hall and outside to see a helicopter approaching. She waved her arms frantically, shouting at the top of her voice as it neared and neared, and came overhead. It must see her, it *must*! It seemed to dip, as if in acknowledgment of her cries, and then came down lower. Sally caught her breath. They had seen her—and it was going to land. Lower and lower—and now behind the house. Fleet of foot, she ran round the villa through the trees to the back, saw it hovering only feet above the ground, then come to rest like a giant mosquito on a large sandy patch. The blades whirred and clicked, and then were still.

'Oh, thank you, thank you!' she called as she ran towards it, to see the door opening slowly, to see the man jumping down.

'Please help——' she began, and the words died in her throat. The man was Luke Vilis, and he was alone. She was dusty and scratched from her headlong flight through the trees at the side of the villa, and she felt the sting of the scratches as she stood there numbed and bemused, and watched him walking towards her.

'Thought someone had come to rescue you?' he said mockingly. 'You made a beautiful picture standing there waving your arms about. Sorry to disappoint you, but I told you you wouldn't get away——'

She hit him as hard as she could, right across his face, and he grabbed her arm as she took it away and swung her round. 'Don't ever do that again,' he grated, 'or you'll be sorry. Now, get back to the house.'

'I won't!' she shouted. 'I'm not going ...'

'Oh yes, you are.' His grip on her arm tightened. 'Move!'

'I—ouch! You're——'

'Then walk. I want some food, and you're going to prepare it.' He pulled her along, as he had done from the boat, and Sally, having no choice, too shocked with sheer disappointment, followed.

In the kitchen he turned to her. 'Dinner,' he said.

'The freezer's well stocked, go and get something out and we'll eat.'

She stood facing him. 'I won't! I'll starve before I'll do anything for . . .'

'Listen,' he said, 'and listen carefully. The sooner you start to do as you're told, the sooner you'll make life easier for yourself. Now, do I make myself clear? By every act of defiance you are only prolonging your stay here—and that's a promise.'

She looked at him silently, digesting the words. She saw his strength, and she knew now why she had been frightened of him the first time she had seen him. This was a man who did precisely what he said he would, a man who would not be deflected by anything from what he chose to do, and she knew too that for the first time in her life she had met her match. The knowledge was disturbing. Sally took a deep breath, then in a quieter voice, she said: 'I don't know much about cooking.'

'You wouldn't, would you? I bet you've never had to do any, so now's the time to learn.' His eyes were cold and as hard as ice chips. 'And I'll teach you. I'll teach you a lot of other things as well. I'll teach you humility. I'll make you regret all the selfish things you've ever done . . .'

'You'll teach me?' she gasped. '*You* who robbed my uncle—how can you . . .'

'You know nothing.' His voice was perfectly calm, something she should have recognised as a danger signal, because it was the more deadly for that. 'So I advise you to watch your tongue. I have a fine temper when I get going, so don't make me lose it. Now, the freezer. This way.' She followed him out of the kitchen and into a room that held freezer, washer, and work bench. He opened the deep chest freezer and looked outside. 'Hmm, I think a pizza, and then some scampi.' He began to get them out, and handed her the two packets. 'I like my scampi deep fried in batter, okay?' She stared at him silently. 'I'll show you how to make the batter. Meantime, the pizza goes in the cooker. See? I'm being easy on you as it's your first night. Not a lot of elaborate cooking.'

'You're all heart,' she said with feeling, and he laughed.

'The girl has a sense of humour! Well, well. That and intelligence. You know, I might find this more entertaining than I thought.' He looked at her for a moment. 'And you're quite attractive too, in a hard way.' He stroked her cheek. 'Good skin, good teeth, hair just as I like it.' He ran his fingers through her hair, and Sally stood there, controlling the urge to hit him, biting back the words she knew she would regret if she dared to say them, and Luke Vilis nodded: 'Yes, you're learning.' Then he smiled, ever so softly. He took his hand away from her hair, and Sally found her voice.

'You can't change other people. Do you think you can? Do you think it's that easy?' She lifted her chin. 'Well, you're wrong. I have to put up with your insults because I'm stuck here with you and I know you're twice as strong as me—so I'll learn this much. I'll shut up and I'll do as I'm told, and then you'll let me go back to Adelana—*when* will you let me go, by the way? Is there a points system for good behaviour? Do tell me, then I'll know how long I've got—and then, when I get back, you'll be sorry.'

His eyes narrowed. 'Will I? And how will you do that?'

'You'll see. Just tell me what I've got to do now and I'll do it. You'll get your scampi, don't worry.'

'Right.' He began to open various cupboards, and in a few moments there were dishes and bowls, flour and milk and eggs waiting on a working top. He went out of the room to return with a brightly covered cookery book. This he slammed down on the top. 'It's all yours,' he said. 'I'm going to have a shower. Don't forget the pizza goes into the oven now.' And he walked away towards the door.

'But——' she was startled, 'you said you'd show me now . . .'

'I changed my mind. You're intelligent—get on with it. I won't be long.' He went out of the kitchen. The silence washed in after him, and Sally looked at what she had to do, then at the door, and her mouth tightened. She waited until she heard the sound of running water, then crept to the door, paused, listened briefly, then ran out of the villa and towards the helicopter. She had no idea of how to fly one, but she was going to have a jolly good try. As she ran swiftly through the trees she desperately tried to recall her one and only ride in a helicopter, a few years previously. She had watched the pilot then, fascinated by the array of dials and clocks, and by the confident way he had handled the controls. It wouldn't be easy; it might be impossible, but if she could possibly escape

—or even make radio contact with someone, anyone, who could help . . .

It waited, huge and silent, and she scrambled up the steps and inside, her heart beating wildly. This was it. No panic, calmness was essential. She sat in the pilot's seat of the cabin and looked at the dazzling display before her, and her heart sank. It was no use. She wouldn't know where to begin. But there was the radio, and she was going to try. She picked up the headphones, pressed a couple of switches, heard a faint burst of static, and her heart lifted. In a low, urgent voice, she began: 'Hello, hello, is anybody there?' She began to twiddle the knobs, and faint voices and morse signals emerged from the distance, and she began to repeat: 'Mayday, Mayday . . .'

Crash! Violence erupted in one split second as the door to the cabin was flung wide open. Luke Vilis's hand clamped down on the switches, the headset was torn from her, and she was pulled—literally—out of her seat to face him. In a fury of despair and frustration she pushed out at him with all her strength, sent him flying out of the door—only he took a grip on her so that she went with him. They landed in a flying tangle of feet and legs and arms on the ground, and for a moment Sally struggled violently but vainly to escape.

Then she was helpless, pinned to the ground by a furious man whose weight crushed her, knocking the breath from her body as she heard his voice, as if from a distance, harsh and hard: 'By God, you're a fighter. Let's see how you fight *this*!' And his mouth came down on hers with a savage intensity that completely took the last vestiges of her resistance away. Gasping, fighting for breath, she lay there beneath him, feeling the hardness of his body against hers, the power of his legs and arms, and the strength of his treacherous mouth. His fingers were in her hair, and she knew she was utterly helpless. It was the most frightening sensation she had ever experienced in her life. The violence of his actions was no less terrifying, as images of rape flashed into her mind, and of how she had always thought rape was impossible—now she knew differently. If he had chosen at that moment to make love to her, she would not have been able to do a thing about it. She began to feel faint, fainter—and then, suddenly, everything was subtly changed. There was no instant of awareness, just a shifting of balance, a vague stirring within her, as his embrace became less savage, and his lips, the warm mouth pressing down on hers, gentler. Warmth filled her body. Almost without being aware of what she was doing, she began to respond to his excitement, and, as her heart pounded unbearably, sensed that he knew it. She stirred beneath him, now able to move more easily, and her whole body tingled with the warmth and hardness of his.

Abruptly, and nearly as violently as in the helicopter, he moved, lifted his weight from her, and looked down at her. His eyes had gone darker with passion, were shadowed and deep, and a pulse beat strongly at his throat. And Sally knew in that moment of timeless awareness that if she moved in a certain way, if she said certain words, nothing would stop him from making love to her. The warning bells rang in her head. She took a deep shuddering breath, and a measure of control came back to her. It wasn't going to be like this, not the first time. 'Is this what you brought me here for?' she whispered, 'to rape me?'

He pulled her to her feet and stood facing her, and she saw that the savage excitement was still within him, but he too had found control. A muscle worked in his jaw, and for a moment he didn't speak. Then: 'But it wouldn't have been rape, would it?' She saw the hard mockery in his eyes, on his face, saw the contempt on his lips, and she reached out to strike him, to wipe the expression from his face, and he caught and held her arms.

'I've already warned you—don't,' he grated. She arched her back in an effort to free herself, and kicked his shin.

'You beast!' she said, trembling. 'You're nothing but an animal——'

'A human animal, yes—like you.' The grip tightened subtly on her arms. 'Don't worry, I've no taste for rape.' Then he paused, and added very softly, so that she could scarcely hear the words: 'But I shall make love to you before I've finished with you.' He turned away after releasing her. 'Now back to the house.'

'You won't get near enough to try again,' she spat back. 'I'll see to that!'

He half turned, turned and looked at her in a way that made warmth flood her face.

'Didn't you know? I'm like you—I always get my own way.' And he strode off, leaving her to follow him back to the villa. She had no choice. There was no escape, and she had suddenly realised she was starving. Her legs were still weak, and she walked at a slower pace than he, and she wondered when, if ever, the nightmare would end.

Luke Vilis pushed his plate away from him. 'At least you didn't ruin the pizza. I suppose we must be thankful for small mercies.' His eyes met hers across the table. 'Didn't you know you're supposed to get the oil very hot before adding the scampi?'

Sally looked back at him. 'They—they didn't taste too bad to me.' She was surprised at the defensive note in her voice. As if she had to apologise to *him* for anything!

'I've had worse. Not often, but you'll learn—in time.' The last two words sank in slowly and she bit her lip. Now was the moment to ask an important question.

'My uncle will be worried about me—and my aunt.' She added that as an afterthought. 'Are you going to let them know where I am?'

'And have them charging across to the rescue? Do you think I'm a fool?'

'But you can't——' she began, then saw his face, and stopped. Rosa's words came back to her: 'If you upset him in any way, you'll be out of here so fast your feet won't touch the ground.' And Uncle Alistair was ill, very ill, but didn't know it. She closed her eyes in despair. Dear God, this could kill him, she thought. 'You must,' she said. 'Somehow—I don't care what you tell them, just as long as they know I'm *safe*, that's all.'

'You're concerned?' He sounded surprised.

'Yes.' She had made a promise to Rosa that she must keep, but somehow she had to impress on Luke Vilis the urgency of the situation. 'I'm very fond of my uncle—I can't—not let him know something.' She looked down at the empty plate in front of her, and swallowed. 'C-can't you tell him we're old friends or something, and I just d-decided to go off with you?' She was no longer in control of the situation. She felt unsure of herself, and her voice trembled, but there was nothing she could do about it.

He laughed. He even sounded genuinely amused. 'Don't you think that would bother them even more?'

'No. Please.' She looked up, and her eyes were bright with shaming tears. She hadn't cried for years, but she felt it now. 'Rosa won't be surprised—she more or less told me what she thought of me when I came.' It was humiliating to have to speak thus, but Sally had a compulsion to make Luke Vilis understand. 'She'll explain to him. And he'll accept——'

He nodded. 'Ah, I see. You mean she has no illusions about you? A sensible woman. She'll be the making of him, perhaps.'

If only you knew, she thought. Oh God, if only you knew the truth. 'Then—will you?'

He rose to his feet. 'I'll think about it. You can make me some coffee and take it out to me. I'll be on the verandah. Black, two sugars.' He went out. Sally cleared the plates and put water on to boil. Hot, black, two sugars—she must get it right. She must—she *must* humour him. The water boiled, she made two coffees and carried them outside to the wooden verandah with its spectacular views of island, rocks, and sea, and set his cup and saucer before him. He eyed her speculatively. 'Sit down. Drink your coffee.' She sat down and waited for him to speak again. 'So. You're very fond of your uncle, are you?'

'Yes.'

'And you hate me because he hates me?'

She looked up quickly, sensing a trap, but his face was bland. He was smoking a cigar, and the smoke drifted lazily upwards in the still air, and he waited for her answer.

'What do you expect me to say?' she asked.

'The truth. I ask nothing more than that. Don't be afraid to say it. I loathe liars.'

'Yes. All right, yes, I do hate you. And not only because of what you did to him, but for abducting me as well. Does that satisfy you?' Some of her spirit had returned. He was playing with her, as a cat plays with a mouse, and she was weary of it all.

He nodded as if satisfied. 'Well, that's a truthful answer anyway.' He picked up his coffee cup and drank some. 'Hmm, not too bad.'

Sally couldn't help the huge sigh of relief. His eyes were upon her, and there was a look in them she didn't like, and she wondered what was to come next, sensing something, feeling something in the very atmosphere around them. Then it came. 'Tell me,' he said softly, and his voice gave no hint of the shock that was to come, 'are you a virgin?'

Sally's head jerked up, colour flooding her face. 'What?' she gasped.

'You heard. Are you? Just answer yes or no—I

shan't beat you whatever you say, I just want to know —and I'll know whether you're lying.'

'You have no right to——' she began.

'If you want me to let your uncle know you're safe, you would do better to answer me now.'

She took a deep breath. 'Yes,' she said at last, and waited for his laughter. But none came.

'I believe you are. Why?'

She jumped to her feet. 'I'm not staying here to answer stupid questions from you!' and she stalked away from him into the kitchen. Luke followed her and swung her round to face him.

'I said I want to know why. You must admit it's very unusual, not to say rare, in this permissive day and age, and especially in the company *you* keep.' He paused, and his hands were more gentle on her arms. 'Why do you tremble?'

'At your insolence,' she breathed. 'Why should it be any business of yours anyway? Are you?'

He laughed. 'No, but I sensed you were when we had our little scene outside the helicopter—and I was intrigued——'

'Then don't be. Now you know, I hope you're satisfied.'

'Not yet. I still want to know why.'

She looked straight into his eyes. 'Then I'll tell you, shall I? Then perhaps you'll l-leave me alone. B-because I've never met a man I've wanted to make love to me. Laugh if you like—go on. Oh yes, I know it's odd, in this day and age, as you said, and I enjoy kissing, and all the trimmings, as much as any woman, but——' she stopped, and now her whole body was shaking, and she would have fallen had he not held her.

'But?' he enquired softly yet inexorably.

'My—mother has been married four times. She's an actress, you know, a very famous and beautiful one.' She managed a brave smile to hide the trembling mouth. 'And she's had many lovers as well—and I've seen her with them, and met them, and I hate—I hate——' She couldn't go on.

'You hate men?'

Alarm flared in her eyes. 'No! I didn't say that! I——'

'But you do. Is that why all those conquests of yours? Do you lead them on so that you can then——'

She wrenched herself from him. 'Leave me alone,' she sobbed. 'Leave me——' the tears coursed down her face, and she didn't see the expression on Luke Vilis's face. He touched her, but not in any way violently.

'Sit down. I'll bring in your coffee.'

She fumbled for the chair and sat in it, her mind in a turmoil, but already fighting back for self-possession. No one had ever seen her like that before, and she was afraid of the strength of her own reactions to his words. 'Here, drink it,' he ordered. 'I have a proposition to make to you.'

She drank the hot sweet coffee and looked up at him, tears dried, face under control again. 'What is it?'

'That's better. I prefer you when you're your haughty self again. It's this. How would you like to see your uncle living in his old villa again, with money, and his Rolls-Royce, and his servants?' He cocked an eyebrow after the silence that followed. 'Well? Lost your tongue?'

She shook her head. 'Of course I would—but how? I don't understand——'

'You will. I'm prepared to restore all the things I "stole"—and I use the word advisedly—in return for —you.'

You. It was the way he said it. Sally felt as if she was gaping at him like a fish out of water. Then something filtered through, and she shuddered. 'Oh no— you mean——' she shook her head, fighting nausea.

'I don't think you do know what I mean—not exactly. Do you?'

'You want to m-make love to me . . .'

'I want to marry you.'

The words seemed to fall like stones into a pool, and the ripples of them widened until they filled the room, echoing and re-echoing—I want to marry you—marry you—marry you . . .

'You're mad!' she gasped.

'On the contrary, I'm perfectly sane. You will marry me, and live here with me, and be my wife—and your uncle will be happy again.' He paused. 'But if you say yes, simply to get away from here, and then retract, you will regret it, so think carefully before you speak. For I will punish not only you, but him—I will see that life on Adelana becomes so uncomfortable that he will be forced to move away. And I can do it. I own practically everything on it—the shops, cafés, boats——'

'And if I say no?' she asked, hardly daring to breathe.

He shrugged. 'You simply stay here for as long as I want you to.'

'But you promised to let them know . . .'

'I didn't promise, I said I'd think about it. And then I had this idea that was too good to miss.' He smiled. 'So—your answer?'

'Why?' she whispered. 'Why?'

'Two reasons. One—and most important—I shall rid myself of someone who is making life—er—difficult for me.' He smiled thinly. 'And I'm sure you'll know all about breaking off relationships. And two—I shall have my sweet revenge completed. That's all.' He looked at her. 'Well?'

Sally didn't meet his eyes. She was caught, and she knew it. One thing *he* didn't know, would never know until it was too late. It would, mercifully, be only for a few months, a year at most. For her uncle's sake, the one person in the world she loved, she could do it. Then when he died she would walk away without a backward glance, and with head held high. It would be a sacrifice to marry Luke, the first in her selfish young life, but she would make it. What was a year out of a lifetime? 'All right,' she said. 'I agree.'

# CHAPTER FOUR

LUKE VILIS stood up. 'Come,' he said, 'to the telephone with me.'

'It's not working,' said Sally. She felt as if she were in a dream.

'It was disconnected,' he said, quite gently for him. 'Did you think I would leave it for you to phone after I'd gone?'

She followed him into the room off the hall and watched him plug the telephone wires into a hidden socket in the wall. She felt sick. If only she had *looked* before, it would all have been over by now ...

'Hello.' He had picked up, dialled, been connected. So easy, so very easy. 'Mrs Herrick? This is Luke Vilis—no, don't hang up, please, I have something very important to say, something that concerns you and your husband—and Sally.'

She could almost feel Rosa's astonishment and anger at the other end of the line. Sally clenched her hands tightly, willing herself to control. 'We would like to come and see you this evening——' A pause. 'Yes, Sally is here with me. Do you want to speak to her? No, I see——' Another pause. 'I assure you, Mrs Herrick, I have no intention of upsetting your husband in any way. In fact I think he will be pleasantly surprised—and you too, of course.'

Then he waited, and Sally could hear Rosa's voice faintly from the other end of the telephone. The words were inaudible, the tone was clear. Yet Luke Vilis's face gave nothing away. He listened expressionlessly. Then he spoke:

'About nine-thirty, then. Goodbye.' He put the phone down, then turned to Sally. 'We're leaving soon. I shall have a shower now—the one I didn't have before. Would you like one?'

'I'll wait until I get home,' she said.

He smiled. 'This will soon be your home,' and he walked out of the room and left her alone. She sat down on the cane settee and put her face in her hands. She wondered how she was going to bear the next few months.

It was Rosa who opened the door, Rosa who, icy-faced, took them into the lounge and closed the door firmly behind her. 'Sit down, Mr Vilis,' she said. 'I may as well tell you now, Alistair is in bed. He has had a sleeping draught, and I made sure he didn't know who had phoned before, because until you've told me everything of why you're here, and what Sally'—here her eyes flickered over to where Sally still stood by the window—'is doing with you when as far as I'm aware she didn't even know of your existence two days ago—I am not prepared to let you see or talk to my husband. Do I make myself clear?'

You had to hand it to her, thought Sally. She knew how to put herself across. She waited with a kind of detached interest for Luke Vilis to explode. He merely nodded, as if he had expected no less. 'Then

I'll tell you, Mrs Herrick.' He looked quite formidable, ruthless, yet it was tempered with the magnificent confidence he always possessed. 'Sally has agreed to marry me, and I have decided that Mr Herrick and you can have your villa, your Rolls—and the sum of sixty thousand pounds the day we are married. Is that clear enough for you?'

'My God!' Rosa, ashen-faced, sank into a chair. Then she looked up at Sally. 'Is this true—what he says?'

'Yes.'

'Why? You don't even know him——'

'Does that matter?' Luke cut in.

Rosa looked across at him. 'Sally's old enough to know what she's doing, I suppose. But why should a man like *you*'—she filled the last three words with fine contempt—'want to help us—after what happened?'

'Because,' he said quietly, 'I may not be the man you seem to think I am.'

Oh yes, you are, thought Sally, but said nothing. 'I don't know what to say,' said Rosa. 'I'll have to think about it.'

'There's nothing to think about, Mrs Herrick,' he answered. 'Sally doesn't need anyone's permission to marry. All you have to do is say whether or not you want the money.'

'Money?' Rosa's eyes blazed as she glared at him. 'Of course we want the money you stole, and the other things . . .'

'No.' His voice was not raised, yet it effectively stopped Rosa. 'No, I did not steal anything from your husband. I don't know what he told you, but whatever it was, he has clearly painted the wrong picture. If I could speak to him . . .'

'No! He'll be asleep now. And in any case he's not been well. This would be a shock. I'll have to break it to him gently.'

Luke stood up. 'Then I might as well go. He is the one I wanted to see, when can I do so?'

There was an instant of electric silence, then Rosa said, more quietly: 'Perhaps—in the morning—say about noon, when I've had a chance to talk to him.'

'Very well. I shall be here.' He turned to Sally. 'And the wedding will be the day after tomorrow, at ten o'clock.' She went icy all over. That was it. Ten o'clock, day after tomorrow, one wedding. Before she could speak, could say, but suppose they don't accept? he had gone out as quietly as he came, and the front door closed after him with the barest click, then all was silent.

Rosa had put her hand to her forehead, and after a few minutes she spoke, her voice muffled. 'Get me a drink, Sally, please.'

'What? Whisky? Rum?'

'Anything, just anything.'

Sally poured a measure of rum into a glass and added ice from the ice bucket and handed it to her aunt. Rosa looked up. She was white with shock. 'I think,' she said slowly, 'that you'd better tell me.'

'There's nothing much to tell,' said Sally, 'except what Luke told you—that's it in a nutshell. I'm marrying him the day after tomorrow.' It sounded unreal even as she said it. 'Can I have a drink too, please?' she asked.

Rosa nodded. 'Help yourself. You can't marry a man you've only just met—or can you? Is it his money?'

If only she knew! Sally managed a sphinx-like smile as she raised her glass to her lips. There was no way in which she could begin to tell Rosa the whole humiliating truth. 'Mmm, aren't I a clever girl?' she said lightly.

'And a fast worker.' Rosa's eyes were hard.

'If you like. Does it matter to you?'

'Nothing you do can ever matter a damn to me—I thought I told you that the day you arrived.' Rosa stood up, and she was calmer now. 'Just so long as Alistair isn't hurt. Do you understand that?'

'Oh, absolutely.' Sally's eyes sparkled. 'You make yourself perfectly clear, dear aunt. So you'll take the money, and the villa, and the . . .'

'We'll take back what belongs to us, yes. And I'll do the talking to Alistair in the morning, not you.'

'I wouldn't expect it otherwise.'

'And when you get married I hope you don't expect an elaborate reception.'

'I expect nothing, thank you.' Sally took a deep breath. 'I've a white dress in my luggage—as far as I'm concerned, that's all I need.'

'A *white* dress?' The smile on Rosa's face said all that her words did not.

'Yes,' said Sally very quickly, 'a white one. And I'll wear it. Now I think I'll go to bed—I've had a very tiring day.'

'I can well believe that,' agreed Rosa sweetly. 'You have, after all, managed to hook a millionaire.' And she watched Sally, who walked towards the door as if stunned. A millionaire, she thought. How very *funny*! At least it would have been, in different circumstances. The dream of most ambitious girls' lives come true— yet she, and only she, knew the truth of it all, the real reasons and there was nothing even faintly amusing about *them*.

Yet when morning came, and Sally went out to the verandah on which her uncle sat, she knew for the first time a sense of satisfaction at what she had been forced into doing. He took her hand, and the gratitude and love in his eyes was something heartwarming to see.

'I don't know why, or how—I don't know anything —but you've just managed to make your uncle feel about eighteen again. Sally, oh, Sally, you must be a witch!'

She smiled softly. 'Possibly. The main thing is—are you happy?'

'Of course. Why, we can go to England for a holiday now—something we just haven't been able to afford for years—and I can see a specialist friend I know. He might be able to tell me why I feel so darned tired all the time—though Rosa's news has been a tonic that's done me more good than any medicine.'

But Sally wasn't listening. A wave of realisation washed over her. Her uncle might be *cured*—it could be possible. They would be able to afford the top medical treatment in the world now—and if he *was*—why, she could leave Luke even sooner than she had hoped, for Alistair and Rosa would be independent . . .

'I'm sorry, what did you say, Uncle?' She had been lost in her dream world. It would work out all right, she knew that now.

'You were miles away. I said Rosa seemed a bit startled by the news of your marriage—and I must confess I was too. Are you—er—sure you're doing the right thing?'

She looked at him, cheeks glowing. 'Oh *yes*! Quite sure.' And just at that moment, she was.

He relaxed, patted her hand. 'That's all right, then. Only Vilis is a tough customer, a ruthless man——' Oh, I know that, she thought, don't I know it, 'and I want you to be happy.'

But you'll never know why I did it, she thought, as she looked into her uncle's face, and I'll never tell you. It's the first time I've ever really done anything for anyone else. Perhaps even Rosa might not dislike me so much if she knew the truth. Not that I care, she added silently to herself. Yet, strangely enough, she did.

'You don't need to worry about me,' she said lightly. Then, on a more serious note: 'Did he really rob you?'

Her uncle's face grew shadowed, and—could there have been the slightest trace of embarrassment there? 'It's a long story,' he answered.

'And can't you tell me?' she asked, voice soft.

'If I don't, he will.' He looked at her then. 'I know what Rosa thinks—oh, Sally, I've been a foolish

man in my time, and I suppose I did give her a highly
coloured version of things—but it was only because I
love her so much that I didn't want to lose her. You
see, years ago, I had a gambling streak in me—but I
think you already know that, don't you?' She nodded,
and leaned over to clasp his hand.

'Go on.'

'I didn't change when I moved here, ten years ago.
I'd always been lucky—but my luck was running out,
only I was too foolish to see it. There's a casino on a
neighbouring island, a real tourist attraction. I used
to fly over at weekends—this was before I met Rosa,
of course, and spend the entire time playing poker or
roulette, sometimes winning sometimes losing, but
never doing anything stupid, until one time,' he
paused, 'I must have been mad, I know that now. I'd
got in deeper than I thought. The owner of the casino
tried to warn me off, told me I didn't know what I
was doing, but I thought I did. I lost everything, all
I had in the world, on a turn of a card. If I'd won, I'd
have been wealthy beyond reckoning, and I was
blinded by greed.' He stopped, and Sally, sensing his
distress, said quietly:

'Don't tell me any more if you don't want to.'

He shook his head. 'I must, now I've begun. I asked
for time—to recoup my losses, to save my villa and the
Rolls, and the owner gave it me. So I played the stock
market in a desperate attempt to make more money
—and it all went wrong. I was penniless. Then Rosa
came into my life like some angel, and we were married within weeks of meeting. I lived still in the villa,
and drove the Rolls, and on the surface everything was

perfect.' He leaned back in his chair. 'Oh God, I've been a stupid man! If only I'd met her earlier. But I didn't, and my debt had to be paid, so I paid it. We moved out of the villa into this bungalow, and Rosa brought her own car, which you've seen, and now we live very simply, very quietly.' He looked at her. 'And I suppose I don't need to tell you who the casino owner is, do I?'

'Luke?'

He nodded. 'Yes.'

She closed her eyes. 'Oh, no!'

'One thing I never told Rosa—I should have, but my pride wouldn't let me. He gave me this bungalow, and he returned some of the money I'd gambled away —just enough to live on. There was no legal or moral obligation for him to do so, but he did. And I suppose, because of that, I've hated him ever since. It's a strange fact of life, Sally, but you sometimes grow to loathe the person you're obligated to. It was like accepting charity, a bitter pill to swallow for me. And that's the story. Not a pleasant one, but the truth.'

'But wouldn't he have given you more time, if you'd asked him?' she said, knowing in her heart how useless it would have been. 'He has so much—he must have known you were ruined . . .'

He sighed. 'I have a stiff-necked pride. It's something that runs in the family—an inability, if you like, ever to admit being in the wrong. He—Luke—had already warned me off before that weekend—and I wasn't about to take advice from any young whippersnapper, as I saw him. He runs the casino fairly, let's be quite honest about that. Even an old fool like me

knew that. But a debt is a debt. Do you think, if
people win, they'd like it if Luke asked them to wait
months for their winnings?'

'No, of course not. But ...'

'Sally,' he said softly, 'you're going to marry him.
Whose side are you on?'

She was silenced by that. How could she tell him?
She shook her head. 'I suppose I do sound silly. Of
course I can see it all now. And thank you for telling
me. But—one thing—won't it make you hate him all
the more for what he's going to do now?'

'I've learned sense since I married Rosa. And anyway,' he chuckled, 'he'll be my nephew, won't he? So
it'll be keeping it in the family.'

Sally stood up, bent, and kissed her uncle's forehead. 'You're right. I'd better go in now and have a
shower and look out what I'm to wear tomorrow—for
my wedding.'

He caught her hand. 'You're sure you're doing the
right thing?' Anxiety was in his eyes and on his face.

Sally laughed. 'Sure? Of *course* I'm sure! I couldn't
be more happy!' and she gave him a brilliant smile,
turned and walked back into the bungalow before he
could see the real expression on her face.

He watched her go, puzzled.

The call came at nine the following morning. Rosa
took it, and called Sally, 'It's for you.' She knew who it
was, of course. There was no one else she knew on
the island.

'Sally?'

'Yes.'

'It's Luke. A car will be coming for you in half an hour. You'll be ready?'

'Of course.'

'And—your aunt and uncle, will they be coming to the wedding?'

'I——' she had to clear her throat, 'yes, they will.'

'Right. Goodbye for now.' He hung up. Sally put the telephone down, and the nervousness she had tried so hard to hide since yesterday welled up inside her. He made it sound like a business transaction, she thought suddenly—and in a bizarre way, that was precisely what it was.

'Are you all right?' Rosa had been standing in the doorway.

'I'm fine,' Sally lied. 'Just fine. There's a car coming for us in half an hour.'

'I'll tell Alistair.' Rosa turned away, hesitated, then turned back. 'You look very nice, Sally.' It was the first kind thing she had ever said, and Sally's eyes filled with tears. I don't need you to be nice to me, she thought. Not now.

'Thank you.' She looked down at her dress, so that Rosa wouldn't see her face, and Rosa went silently out, leaving her alone. Sally stroked the skirt, which was long, nearly to her ankles, and wondered if it was really suitable for a wedding. But she had no alternative, and in any case, she thought, there will only be the four of us. But there she was wrong.

She crossed to the mirror. No, it didn't look too bad at all; of off-white cheesecloth, the blouse top was simple, with mere touches of bright embroidery at the waist. She looked slender and fragile. She also looked pale. She opened her bag, applied more lipstick, then very gently smoothed a whisper of it on her cheeks. There, that was better. She even *felt* better. She turned away from the glass and went over to the window to await the car. She saw the long black limousine snaking up the short drive, watched the driver get out and walk towards the front door, and her mouth went dry with apprehension. It shouldn't be like this, she thought. I never wanted it to be like this. But she had committed herself to a course of action, and there was no way out. The bell chimes sounded faintly, and she heard voices and then Rosa came in.

'It's here,' she said. 'You're quite ready?'

'Yes.' Sally's voice came out as an inaudible whisper, and Sally repeated it. Rosa's face softened slightly. 'I've been hard on you, Sally—and I had my reasons, and I make no apology, but this is your wedding day. It's come as a big surprise, not to say a shock, to both of us that everything's happened so swiftly. But you've made Alistair very happy—and therefore me too—and we'll have no money worries, thanks to you—or rather, Luke.' She paused, and it seemed that she was searching for the right words. Then she looked into Sally's eyes, and took her hands. 'I hope you'll both be very happy. I mean that sincerely.'

For a moment they stood there wordless, then Sally's precarious self-control snapped. A huge sob was wrenched from her, and Rosa immediately put her arms round her.

'Oh, don't cry—please don't cry. This is the most important day of your life—ah! I know, it's nerves.'

She gave her a brisk motherly shake. 'Tsh, you'll ruin your make-up—and do you want to go into church with a red nose, hey?' She chuckled, and suddenly, absurdly, Sally was laughing too. Slightly shakily, but laughter nevertheless.

Rosa produced a clean handkerchief from her bag. 'Here, dab your face—that's it, no damage done. Now, keep the hanky. Let's go. Alistair's waiting in the car.'

'Thank you.' Everything was safe again. Tears dried away, her cheeks now naturally pink from the crying. It wouldn't happen again. Sally walked steadily towards the hall, then out to the waiting car. She had expected only the four of them to be there, but there were crowds, lining the path to the small white church, and crammed inside, a colourful throng of islanders. And there was more—what seemed like dozens of cameramen waiting for them, and the flashbulbs like bright stars, dazzling Sally as she stepped out, causing her to look back at Rosa and Alistair in alarm.

'What——?' But they were as puzzled as she, that was obvious. Then into the church. She remembered nothing of the brief service, only a kind of numbness spreading inside her that mercifully prevented her from thinking about what was happening. As in a blur more photographs outside, getting into a car, being whisked away to a large building, going inside, a maid stepping forward to guide her to a large and beautiful bedroom, saying softly to Sally: 'I'll be back in a few minutes, Mrs Vilis, to take you into the reception. Mr Vilis will be with you in a moment.'

Mrs Vilis. That was her name now: Mrs Vilis. Not Sally Herrick any longer. Benumbed, she sat at the dressing table and picked up the comb to tidy her hair, and his voice—her husband's voice—came from the doorway: 'Very nice, Mrs Vilis. You did very well. Are you ready to meet your guests yet?'

She turned to face him. 'Guests?'

'For our wedding breakfast. You didn't think we'd be married and then creep away for a coffee and tea-cakes somewhere, did you?'

'I don't know what I thought,' she answered. 'But the crowds—there must have been a hundred people at the church—and cameras—they were taking my photograph.'

'A hundred and nineteen, to be precise—and taking photographs is usually what men with cameras do. Especially at weddings.'

She looked into his eyes. 'Why?'

He lifted a dark eyebrow. 'So that they can go in an album.'

'Dammit! You know what I mean.' Her eyes gleamed. 'You have a reason for everything you do—and you had a reason for this pantomime——'

'Pantomime? Is that how you saw it?' He looked infuriatingly cool—self-possessed, self-satisfied.

'Yes, that's precisely how I see it.' She rose to her feet and walked steadily across the thickly carpeted room towards him. 'For whose benefit? Not, I think, mine.'

'How astute you are.' He grinned crookedly, his voice barely escaping laughter. 'No, not for yours. For someone else's.'

'And that someone else wouldn't by any chance be

the someone who is making life difficult for you, would it?'

'Don't raise your voice, Sally. We don't want our guests to hear us arguing on our wedding morning, do we?'

'I don't give a single damn what your wedding guests think. In fact——' But whatever she had been about to say was lost as he put his arms round her, pulled her towards him, and kissed her soundly on the mouth.

The door opened, and the little maid said: 'Oh! Sorry,' and vanished instantly, closing the door with a firm click. Sally pulled herself away. Her cheeks glowed with colour, and felt as if they were on fire.

'You did that on purpose, didn't you?' she accused.

'To shut you up. Yes.' His blue eyes bored into hers. 'But it's also my right. Don't forget that—wife.'

She took a deep breath. 'This is a marriage of convenience—yours. You gave me no choice, remember?' Her green eyes could meet his and match the coldness in them. 'Don't think you'll have things all your own way.'

'Meaning?' He wasn't angry, merely amused, which was infuriating, and which goaded Sally into words she would have chosen more carefully had she had time. She laughed.

'What do you think I mean?'

'I want you to tell me.' His voice was harder, and without moving from where he stood, he put out his hand and bolted the door. A slight, almost casual act, yet it had the power to chill Sally's blood. 'Well?' he demanded.

'We'll talk later,' she said. 'Everyone's waiting.'

'As you remarked before—damn the guests,' he answered. 'They're all drinking best champagne by now. Do you think they really care about us—or what we're doing? He smiled thinly. 'Use your imagination, darling. They'll think we couldn't wait ...'

'You're being insufferably coarse!'

'Yes? Then I wonder how much worse I can get——' and he moved towards her, pulled her into his arms with no gentleness at all and whispered: 'I'm going to make love to you now. Right now, over there, on the bed.'

'No—I——' She tried to push him away, but his arms were too strong.

'Yes, oh yes.' His eyes gleamed, and had gone darker. 'You know, you excite me when you fight me like that,' and he bent to her neck and began kissing it, his hands travelling over her body in a gentle caress. 'Mmm, very nice. I don't feel hungry at all. I think——'

Sally felt stifled. She couldn't breathe, and her heart was beating so fast that it seemed as if it might suffocate her. 'No, please—no,' she begged.

'Say my name,' he whispered.

'Luke.'

'Say it louder.'

'Luke.' That was louder.

'It doesn't hurt, does it? You'll have to get used to it, just as you'll have to get used to a lot of things about me. And what better time than now?' And he picked her up and began to walk towards the bed.

Everything that had ever happened in life to Sally

faded into insignificance with the enormity of what was happening now. As he set her down on the large circular bed and pushed her down, she found the last remaining vestiges of her strength to push him away.

'Oh *God*! I—I—hate you!' she whispered, trembling.

'You won't when I've finished with you,' he said softly. 'See—now that doesn't hurt, does it—nor that——' she caught hold of his hands.

'My dress—please—the reception——'

'Then take it off. Let me help you,' and he eased his weight from her, sat up—and Sally seized her chance, slid off the bed and ran to the dressing table. She picked up the first thing that came to hand, a large hairbrush, and brandished it.

'I'll hit you with this. I mean it,' she said.

He walked slowly towards her, shrugged, paused, then with the speed of light had snatched the brush from her and flung it into the corner of the room.

'Go and try and pick it up if you dare,' he said. 'And see how far you get. And by God, I swear I'll take you where I catch you.' The amusement had long gone. Big, lean and dangerous, he stood there facing her, and Sally closed her eyes in weariness.

'Do what you want,' she said. 'I—I can't stop you.'

'No fight left?' he mocked. 'Just when I was beginning to enjoy it too.' She waited, but nothing happened. He made no move to touch her, and after a few moments she opened her eyes.

'Let's go,' he said. She looked at him, dazed and unbelieving.

'What did you say?' she whispered.

'Let's go and join our guests, and have a few more photos taken.'

'But—but——'

He smiled. 'Did you think I meant it? *Here?* Oh, dear me, Sally, you're very naïve for a sophisticated twenty-five-year-old, aren't you? I have a little more delicacy than that. I was teasing you.'

'Teasing?' She felt punch-drunk. 'It didn't seem like teasing to me.' And perversely, she felt a wash of humiliation.

'Then you'll soon learn, won't you? Comb your hair, put some lipstick on. We don't want our guests nudging each other, do we?'

'Go to hell!' she said through clenched teeth, and he laughed.

'That's better. You're back to normal, I see. Good. I prefer you like that, not an acquiescent little mouse waiting for a fate worse than death to befall her. It's more fun when we fight.' He took her arm, leading her to the door, unbolted it, and they went out to join the waiting crowd of people in the large room nearby.

Caught in the throng, busily shaking hands with people she had never seen before, murmuring the conventional answers to the conventional greetings, Sally felt as if floating in a dream. Once, she looked across to where Luke stood a short distance away from her. Smooth, smiling, he was like a stranger. The thought came as a sudden shock. He *was* a stranger, and his mood could change in an instant. And he was her husband.

# CHAPTER FIVE

SALLY was alone. Only for a few minutes; soon she would have to go back and join the guests, but for the moment, in the privacy of the bathroom at the hotel, she had time to think. Her thoughts were not happy ones. All her life she had been accustomed to her own way, every whim indulged by a series of nannies and governesses who were very well paid by her mother. And later, when as a young adult the world had been her oyster, that had been only her just due, and she saw no reason why it should ever be otherwise. Now, for the first time in her life, she faced the reality, the stark reality, of it all changing. The irony of it was that she had simply wanted to get away in order not to lose face among her contemporaries. She wondered if any of them had even spared her a thought since her departure, but it no longer seemed to matter.

She looked in the rosy tinted mirror above the wash basin, saw her face, and it seemed to her that she was older. Her eyes were large and luminous in the soft flattering light. She touched her cheeks gently. They burned with inner fire. If she hadn't come—if Rosa hadn't told her about Alistair's illness—if she hadn't perversely wanted to go to the place Rosa didn't want her to go to. If—it could go on for ever. But she had come, and Rosa had told her, and she had gone. And the result had been this. She looked at the gold ring on her left hand and wanted to take it off and fling it across the room. But it was tight; it wouldn't come off, although she tugged at it. It will soon, she vowed.

There was something she had to know. She had to see her uncle, somehow manage a private word with him, and find out if Luke Vilis had kept his word. Sighing, she turned away from the mirror, unlocked the door, and went out to find him.

He was sitting in a quiet corner of the crowded room sipping champagne, Rosa at his side. Sally didn't waste time because she didn't have it to waste.

'Uncle,' she said, 'what Luke promised—before— has he said anything?'

Rosa smiled, and Alistair patted his breast pocket. 'He's kept his word. There's a cheque here—and the deeds of our old villa,' and Rosa opened her handbag and produced a key ring with three keys on.

'I have the keys,' she said. 'The Rolls is waiting outside.'

Then a hand came on Sally's shoulder, and Luke's voice said in her ear, 'I keep my word.'

Sally didn't flinch. It was an effort, but she managed it. She wondered what would happen if she screamed. Wedding nerves, they'd all say, and smile and shrug, and whisper: 'But it'll be all right after tonight . . .'

'Of course,' she answered, and even managed to smile.

'Are you enjoying yourselves?' he enquired, not looking at Sally. 'Is there anything I can get for you?'

It was Rosa who answered. 'No, thanks. We'll be

leaving soon—Luke.' You could tell, thought Sally, that his name didn't come easily to her, but, give her her due, she was acting the part of a happy aunt of the bride superbly.

'As you wish. Would you like someone to drive you?'

'We'll manage. Neither of us have drunk much.' And it was Alistair who, making the effort, added:

'The meal was superb.'

'I'm glad you enjoyed it. Now, if you'll excuse us, Sally and I are leaving in a few minutes. Come along, Sally.'

Sally bent and hugged her uncle. Luke's words brooked no refusal.

'Bye-bye, love—I'll see you soon.' A slight pause, then she turned to Rosa. Rosa stood up and kissed Sally on the cheek.

'Enjoy yourselves.' She sounded as if she meant it.

'We will,' Luke answered. 'Goodbye.'

Two minutes later they were speeding away from the hotel in his car. The window between them and the chauffeur was closed, the car was well cooled with the air-conditioning, and Sally leaned back against the seat. She had always hated being alone, but now she would have given anything to be so.

'Don't you want to know where we're going for our honeymoon?' Luke said.

'As long as we're apart, I don't really mind.' She had answered with the first words that came into her head, and listened to herself with faint horror.

And he laughed. 'There's an old joke on that theme

somewhere. I would have thought you'd be more original, my dear wife.'

'It was the best I could do at a moment's notice,' she answered.

'Then I suppose I mustn't complain. After all——' he paused, 'we have all the time in the world. I'm sure there are a lot of interesting things you can find to say—and do—over the next few weeks.' He reached out and squeezed her hand, and added gently: 'My dear wife.'

'I wish you wouldn't keep calling me that!'

'Does it annoy you?' He looked interested. 'I must remember that.'

'I suppose the photographs will be in your local paper?' she said, changing the subject.

'Not only that. All over the world.'

That effectively silenced Sally, and Luke regarded her with curiosity. 'You did hear, didn't you?' She nodded. 'And you have no interesting comments to make about that?'

'I suppose—I shouldn't be surprised at anything you do,' she said at last.

'No, indeed you shouldn't. And look at it this way. Think of the surprise of all your London friends when they read the papers in a day or so. All your girl friends will be gnashing their teeth——'

'You flatter yourself.' She said it evenly, without expression.

'Do I? I think not. I know all about your kind of life, your type of acquaintances. Wealth is the only yardstick, isn't it?'

'And money doesn't bring happiness,' she said bitterly.

'Ah! At least you've learned something. Well, well, another little gem. My wife is a woman of infinite surprises, I think. How did you find that one out?'

Sally was silent, thinking of her mother, the utterly selfish and ruthless actress who had clawed her way to the top, amassing a fortune, lovers by the score, and yet who was a deeply bitter and jealous woman. And I haven't even told her, she thought in astonishment. It simply never occurred to me ... 'I use my eyes,' she answered flippantly. 'Are *you* happy, with all your wealth?'

'What an odd question to ask a man on his wedding day!'

'You can cut out the comedy. We haven't got an audience now, remember?' She turned to look at him, really look at him properly for the first time since leaving the reception. 'I know how tough and ruthless you are—I've seen that for myself. I don't know how old you are, or where you were born, or even how you made your money—but I'm willing to bet you're not contented——'

'Who is?' The blue eyes that could be as cold as ice, as dark as passion, or as hard as steel, surveyed her, now amused. 'I drive myself, I work hard, I succeed—and I always get what I want.'

'Then why,' she asked slowly, because the question was just forming itself in her own mind, had been at the back of it all along, and it was inconsistent with the sheer power of him, 'why are you so frightened of a certain woman—I assume it *is* a woman——' one up to me, she thought, 'that you have to marry *me* to escape her clutches?'

He began to laugh, softly at first, then louder. Rich laughter, bubbling out, then he slapped his knee. 'It took you long enough to get that out,' he managed at last. 'I thought you'd never ask.'

'That's not an answer!' she snapped.

'You'll know the answer when you meet her. If you don't, then you can ask me again.'

'And when will that be?' she asked, tight-lipped.

'Why, dear wife, as soon as she reads the papers.'

'Where—where is she?'

'In Australia—at the moment. Not for much longer, I don't imagine.'

'Does she frighten you?' she asked.

'Do you think anything frightens me?'

'I don't know. We all have our weaknesses. Even—I imagine—you.'

'You know, you're quite a philosopher when you get going, Sally. Who knows, our marriage may prove interesting. No, I can't think of anything that scares me. If I do, I'll let you know.'

'You're too kind.' She turned away and looked out of the window to see them nearing the airstrip. 'We're flying?'

'Yes.'

'In the helicopter?'

'No.'

'Then by plane?'

'What else?'

'With a pilot?'

'Yes—me.'

'Just—just the two of us?'

'Yes. Don't you want to know where?'

She felt sick. All of a sudden she felt ill. For then his revenge would truly begin. Or had it already? 'I'll know when we get there, won't I?' she responded.

'You will. It's the ideal spot for a honeymoon, I promise you that. Softly waving palms, sea and sand and sunshine, and a small place for just the two of us.'

'You make it sound like a holiday brochure,' she said in desperation. 'Why—just tell me why—all this?'

'I like comfort, and luxury, and you'll learn some humility.' He glanced across at her and tipped her chin so that she had to face him. Her eyes were bright. 'I promise you that. I'm looking forward to teaching you.'

'You won't break me.' She glared at him in defiance. 'You'll never do that—do you hear? *Never!*'

His eyes narrowed. 'Keep it up,' he said, deceptively soft-voiced. 'You amuse me when you talk like that.'

'If that's the case, I won't.' She smiled, just as the car slowed to a halt by a small plane standing at the end of the runway. Within minutes they were inside the plane, the car was vanishing in a cloud of dust, and Luke said: 'Sit down and fasten your seat-belt.'

She sat, she obeyed, and she thought over his words. It had happened in the hotel bedroom, before the reception, when he had told her that he preferred her fighting than like some acquiescent little mouse—and it began to sow the germs of an idea at the back of her mind. Perhaps he was a sadist, taking his pleasure only when he had to fight for it. She wondered what kind of man he really was. Complex—that much she already knew. Determined on revenge—and to settle an old score with someone who was presumably an ex-mistress—and doing both things in one dramatic sweep. Sally, feeling better already, smiled to herself. He was not going to get things exactly as he wanted. So far, everything had been going his way. But things could change. And there was always her final stroke, the one he couldn't possibly guess at. She was willing to bet nobody had ever walked out on him. She would wait, she would learn patience, she would even pretend humility—but the final triumph would be hers. And that day was worth waiting for. She looked down at the ring on her wedding finger. She would leave him that—nothing more. But it would be enough.

'The island has no name. It isn't even on the map.' Luke stood on the baking landing strip beside Sally, and looked down at her. 'And no one knows we're here, because no one knows this place is mine.'

It was beautiful, and she caught a glimpse of a green roof through the lush trees, and they were surrounded by the silence that only comes in remote places. A complete and utter stillness and calm. And they were here, just the two of them, and for how long she did not know, had not dared to ask.

'Is there food in?' she asked. 'You could hardly have known you'd be coming here two days ago.'

'In the plane. There's a fridge in the cottage, and a generator, so everything will keep. I told you, I like comfort.'

That remark of his gave her the second idea. I like my comfort too, she thought, as they walked towards the trees, he carrying boxes of provisions, she with her suitcase, but it would be worth suffering just to see his face if the generator broke down—irreparably, and she carefully kept her face straight lest he turn round and catch the gleam in her eyes. There were infinitely more ways of winning battles than direct combat. There was cunning, and subterfuge—and sabotage. Sally knew next to nothing about electric generators, but she intended to learn.

The cottage had only four rooms—kitchen, bathroom, lounge and bedroom. She stood in the cool shaded bedroom with its grey blinds drawn and looked about her. A large bed, the minimum of furniture, wardrobe, dressing table, a chair. She slipped off her white sandals and walked barefoot across cool stone tiles to look in the bathroom, and liked what she saw. Under any other conditions, with two people who loved one another, this place would be heaven to be together in. And Sally, who had never understood what love is, laughed cynically to herself, and Luke's voice came from behind her:

'You find the bathroom *funny*?'

'No.' She turned coolly to face him. 'I had a thought, that's all, and it made me laugh.'

'Ah, a private thought?'

'Yes. But I'll tell you, because it doesn't matter. It came to me that this would be the ideal place for two people in love to be. But I don't suppose you know what love is.'

'Any more than you know, you mean?' His face

changed. 'But I do. I loved a woman very deeply once.'

'The one you're succeeding in ditching? That *is* funny.'

'No. *She's* like you. It was someone else, when I was younger. I know what it's like to love someone, Sally. If you care for another person so much that you know you wouldn't want to go on living if anything happened to them, if, without them, the world is a grey cold place—that's love. And that's how it was for us. Only she died ten days after we were married. She was drowned, and I didn't want to go on living. My world ended on that day, and that's how it's been ever since. So now you know why I'm hard and ruthless—and why nothing is very important to me. Or perhaps you don't. I don't really care either way.' He turned and walked away, out of the bedroom.

He could not have imagined the devastating shock his words were for Sally. She remained where she was, numb and icy, unable to move. In those few sentences he had told her so much. Too much for her to take in. He had been human once, and he had known love, love of a kind that was so rare and priceless that it was not of this world. To most people it never happened at all. She thought—why did he tell me? He couldn't know that that was a more cruel thing to have done than anything else. For just for a brief moment she had glimpsed another world, one that would never be hers. Dear God, she thought, life will never be quite the same again, whatever happens. For she would remember his face, as he had spoken, for the rest of her days. And she saw how empty and shallow her existence had been—was now—always would be.

She—the unknown woman—had been his wife, and Sally wanted very much to know her name. She went out to the kitchen. 'What was her name?' she asked.

He straightened up from the refrigerator, where he had been stacking the food. 'Why do you want to know?' His voice was harsh.

'I just do.'

'Laura. You caught me off guard. I've never told anyone. I shall never mention her again. Nor will you.'

She bit her lip. 'I'm sorry.' She had never apologised before to anyone. She didn't know why she said it then, but it was the only thing to say.

'For what? For me—for her—for the fact that she died?' He turned away from her. 'Don't you know that I don't care? If you were to laugh instead, to gloat, that wouldn't be important either. No one—nothing—can touch me any more.' He turned slowly to face her. 'It's nearly time to eat. I'll finish putting this food away and mix us a drink. You can prepare the food,' he waved his arm. 'I've left everything out that you need.' And with that he bent down to finish his task.

In silence Sally began to prepare the cooked chicken and salad that he had left out. Laura. Laura Vilis. Had she been beautiful? She would have been, of course. She would have the glow, whatever her features, of a woman who is deeply loved, an inner glow that owes nothing to outward appearances, but comes from the spirit, and is rare but unmistakable. And Sally knew she had sensed that, perhaps to a lesser degree, in

Rosa. A glass was put down beside her, interrupting the painful train of thought.

'Thank you.' She didn't turn; she didn't want him to see her face. She picked up the glass and drank long and deep. Then she gasped. 'You—you didn't tell me it was vodka——'

'Only half. And lime juice. Don't tell me you're teetotal?'

'Of course not.' And what did it matter anyway? Her unhappiness was almost total. The whole day itself—and what he had just told her only minutes before. She picked up the glass, and finished its contents. 'May I have another?'

'Sure?' He cocked an eyebrow.

'Quite sure.' That first swallow was already having an effect on her empty stomach. She had scarcely eaten a bite at the reception. Her head felt slightly muzzy, and the sensation was not unpleasant. Perhaps, if she passed her entire honeymoon in a drunken stupor, it might almost be bearable. That thought was nearly enough to make her laugh—nearly.

'There you are.' The glass was full, the chicken and salad were set out neatly on the plates, and she carried them to the table. Before she started to eat, she almost finished the second glass.

'No more for you,' Luke remarked amiably, as he broke a piece of crusty bread in two. 'It wouldn't do to have my bride drunk on our wedding night, would it?'

'Wouldn't it? Surely you'd prefer me more—amenable?'

'So you intend to be?'

'I didn't say that—I said——' But it was becoming difficult to remember what she had said. And in any case she hadn't meant it. She had definitely better watch her tongue. 'This farce—you married me to—to teach me a lesson, and to be rid of—what's her name, anyway?'

'Talitha Gervaise.'

She nearly choked over a piece of chicken. 'You made that up!'

'You'll find out whether I did or not when you meet her.'

'Anyway, her—thingy—you married me to be rid of *her*. And I married you because you blackmailed me into it, and as far as the world is concerned, we're man and wife. But as far as *I'm* concerned we're not. Do I make myself clear?'

'No.' He sipped his drink, and watched her. 'But do continue. Your ramblings intrigue me.'

'Oh, don't be so damned flippant!' she burst out. 'Do you want me to spell it out for you?'

'Yes.'

'All right, I will. This is a marriage in name only.' All her fine and subtle plans were going haywire. But she couldn't do anything about it. Her mind was becoming a confused blur, her head ached, and she was desperately tired; hardly surprising considering how little sleep she had had the previous night, her wedding eve. 'And that's how I want it to stay.'

'Fine. Finished eating?' He said it politely enough, as he stood up with his empty plate. That made her more confused than ever.

'So you agree?'

'No. But I'll always listen carefully to any reasonable opinion—even yours.' She stared at him helplessly. 'Now I'm going to have a shower. You can have one after me. There's water in the tap for washing up.' He walked out.

Perhaps he just wanted someone to wait on him. No, he didn't. He made it quite clear, Sally thought, that there was more, much more than that involved. She found it rather difficult to concentrate, but she carried the plates to the sink and tried to think coherently. What was he going to teach her? Humility? She frowned. Was he going to beat her? No, she shook her head. Whatever else she thought about him—and it was quite a lot, he hadn't the appearance of a man who would hit a woman—yet looks could be deceptive . . .

'And don't waste the water. We have enough, but not to waste.' Luke looked round the door, and Sally caught her breath. He wore nothing save a small towel draped Tarzan fashion round his middle.

'Did you hear me?' She must have been gaping.

'Er—yes.'

'Right.' The tall, splendid-looking animal vanished from view, and Sally blinked. Then, very deliberately, she picked up the bottle of vodka, looked at the level of it and poured herself a generous measure. 'Cheers,' she murmured, and drank it in one swallow. Then she ran water into the bowl and began to wash up, humming a little song, off key, but the notes didn't seem to be coming out right and it didn't matter anyway because she was alone. The room steadied into a gentle swaying as she finished the dishes, so she carefully emptied the water out, picked up a tea towel, looked at it, put her tongue out at it, then flung it down on the plates and wove her way gently into the bathroom. She closed the door behind her, crossed to the shower curtain and flung it open.

'I've come to scrub your back, oh master,' she announced with a slight hiccup, and then giggled at the fantastic funniness of her remark.

Luke turned, startled, and Sally stepped into the shower, took the sponge he was holding out of his hands and began to rub soap on it. The fact that the water was drenching her too didn't register for a moment.

'You little fool,' he said. 'You're absolutely blotto.'

'The best way to be,' she agreed with a giggle, wondering why she felt so deliciously cool all of a sudden. 'Turn round.'

'You're soaked,' he pointed out.

'You just told me that!'

'I mean your dress——' She looked down. How funny it was!

'Never mind, I have to learn humility. This will teach me.'

'Hadn't you better take it off?' he said, and she was surprised to note the change in his voice.

She frowned. 'Hmm—well, if you think—oh dear, there's a zip at the back, I don't think I can reach——' her voice tailed away as she began rubbing vigorously at his chest, watching the soapy lather being washed away with remarkable satisfaction.

'Turn round.' He said it in a voice that held all the authority in the world, and she obediently turned.

'Yes, oh master. Anything you say, oh master——'

The zip slid down, down, down, and she stepped out of the dress and kicked it away. 'Whoops! There you go!' she squealed. Then Luke's arms went around her, and he turned her round to face him again, and pulled her to him. 'Wait,' he said huskily.

She looked up to see his face, a watery blur as the shower cascaded down on to her upturned features, and she felt his hands at her back, undoing the clasp of her bra; a grain of sense stirred within her, and she said: 'Oh! But——'

But his mouth came down on hers, crushing, demanding, and she could no longer speak. Not that she wanted to. She put up her arms, round his neck to hold him to her, and felt the hardness of his body crushing against her, then she felt the water stop, and closed her eyes even tighter to stop the world going round, only it didn't, so that when he picked her up she wasn't aware of what was happening until she was being carried out of the bathroom. She felt the hard bed beneath her, and then she opened her eyes and sighed a little sigh. Luke bent over her, nearer, nearer, and then—and then she knew she had been waiting, subconsciously, for this moment all along, ever since the first instant she had seen him. 'Big, lean and dangerous'—The words, her first thought about him, floated into her mind as his mouth came down again on hers. Only now it was very different, so very different ... 'And all man ...' A cry escaped her, a soft breath of sound. 'Ah ...'

Sally woke up to the soft dawn light, and moved uneasily. For a moment she lay there and wondered where she was, then she heard the steady breathing from beside her, and turned her head to see Luke deeply asleep. A wave of warmth rose through her as she remembered where she was, and recalled how she had got there. She lay very still, lest he waken up, and she remembered ... Everything that had happened from the minute she had walked into the shower went through her mind, like a slow-motion film, and her breathing quickened. Now at last she knew what ecstasy could be, for she had tasted it, and life would never be the same again.

A small sigh escaped her, and Luke stirred in his sleep, and moved his hand, and it touched her. For a moment she lay still, her heart thudding so loudly it seemed that he must hear it, and then, slowly, as if in a continuation of the slow-motion film, his fingers moved, and he caressed her, and turned towards her, and she moved towards him, knowing he was still three-quarters asleep, and touched his chest lightly, stroking it, still lost in the memories. He murmured something she couldn't catch, and his hand went up to her face and smoothed her cheek, and his mouth came upon hers, and their bodies were somehow touching, but now there was no haste, there was time, all the time in the world. His body was warm, so warm, and he was so tender yet demanding, a delicious heady mixture that Sally's senses reeled and she was drowning in a warm sea of pleasure ...

Until afterwards, as she lay in the protection of his arms, her body curled tightly against his, and the word that he had said, that she hadn't heard properly returned to her, and she knew what it was now, as if a veil had been dropped, and it seemed to echo and re-echo in her ears. The word so sleepily murmured had been—'Laura.'

# CHAPTER SIX

HAD he pictured Laura as he made love to her? Had it been Laura's body that he imagined? Sally stood in the kitchen, and knew the final humiliation of all as the chaotic thoughts crowded into her head. And the questions that could never be answered made her shiver helplessly despite the heat of the day filling the room, flooding in with the light of the sun through the open door to the verandah. If he had chosen *that* as her punishment, he could have thought of no finer way to completely have his revenge.

He slept; she had slid out of bed, pulled on a dressing gown, and fled to the kitchen. It was nearly nine, but not for anything would she wake him. Her skin burned where he had touched her, her face was afire with the memory of his kisses, and her ears seemed to hear again the fatal word, Laura. It seemed to fill the whole universe, that one name, the name of a woman long dead, the woman he still loved, probably always would. Sally wanted to escape, but there was no way for her to go. She looked out, then walked on to the verandah, holding her arms tightly across her body, as if for protection.

Luke had his revenge. She had sworn that he would not break her spirit, but he had succeeded all the same—with a lot of help from me, thought Sally, with bitterness. She had practically invited him ... Useless to blame the vodka. It would be easy to do so, but she had no illusions. She had, she supposed, known exactly what she was doing, even as she had swallowed that last drink.

She heard, almost disinterestedly, the familiar drone of a helicopter overhead. She didn't bother to look up. It wouldn't be coming here, for no one knew that they were on the island, and even if they did, who would disturb the happy honeymooners anyway? She waited for the sound to die away so that she could think her thoughts undisturbed, only it didn't. It seemed to be circling round. Sally looked up, but could see nothing. The sound grew louder, louder, until she was nearly deafened. Then—silence, a sudden, all-embracing silence, not a fading away, which could only mean one thing. Someone else had landed on the island.

She should wake him, but she didn't want to. Some instinct of feminine vanity made her go over to the small mirror that hung in a corner of the kitchen. She looked into it and saw her auburn hair, tousled after sleep, framing her face—and it was almost a shock to look at herself, the first time she had done so for many hours. She looked fragile, and there was a new awareness, a softness about her eyes, the green eyes that looked back at her. Faint smudges underneath only accentuated the delicacy of her features, and a slight flush touched her cheeks, and she thought, so this is how I look—now. I've often wondered ...

A woman's voice came from outside, calling Luke's

name, a voice resonant with anger. Sally knew who it must be. She turned away from the mirror, and she was filled with a surge of vibrant strength, so much that it nearly took her breath away. This—this she was ready for. And Talitha Gervaise, whatever, whoever she was, and whoever she thought she was, was about to get the biggest shock of her life. Something's happened to me, thought Sally, something so earth-shattering—and you, Talitha, will never know—that she is as nothing. She pulled the housecoat tightly round her, flicked her hair back from her face, and walked with immense dignity to the door of the cottage and flung it open.

'You'd better come in,' she said.

A smouldering tigress swept past her, brushing her to one side, and Sally watched her pass with quiet amusement. 'He's in the bedroom,' she said. 'If you know where it is.'

The woman turned. Tall, taller than Sally, svelte, dark and fiery-haired, brown eyes gleaming hatred. Sally looked her up and down slowly, then smiled. 'I'll find it,' she spat. 'And then I'll deal with *you*!'

'You don't need to look far,' Luke's voice drawled, and he appeared, clad in a towelling robe and nothing else. The woman whirled round, walked over to him, and reached up her hands to rake his face. He caught and held them, and looked down at her. Then he laughed.

'How on earth did you find us?' he asked.

'Never mind that.' She wrenched her hands free. 'You've made your point, in the most stupid way possible,' the fine dark eyes met Sally's, and the woman gave a throaty chuckle. 'My God!' she exclaimed, 'what a fool you are! All because of a stupid quarrel—we'll go back together, darling, and you'll never want to stray again.' She smoothed the silky black dress she wore, sensuously emphasising the contours of a stunning figure, and almost purred: 'It will be better than before.'

'Excuse me,' Sally murmured, putting her hand to her mouth to hide a yawn, 'I'll just go and make a drink,' and she drifted into the kitchen. There she stood for a moment, and thought. But Talitha knows nothing—for she doesn't know about Laura, and I do, and although she is a strong woman, super-confident of her own sexual powers, I'm sorry for her. For she *is* nothing. She remembered Rosa telling her that same thing—I'm sorry for you, she had said. And now Sally understood. She understood so much that she hadn't before, and the knowledge filled her with a calmness and strength she had never before possessed, and it was enough—more than enough, to enable her to cope with anything that would ever happen.

She opened the refrigerator and took out the jug of orange juice that was covered inside. Each movement was economical and precise, and when they walked into the kitchen, Talitha almost quivering with anger, Luke hard and calm, Sally was able to look at them both with equanimity.

'Orange juice?' she said. 'Or coffee?'

Talitha didn't answer her, Luke said: 'Coffee,' and Talitha turned towards Sally.

'He's mine,' she announced. 'He has been for ages. You don't even know him——'

'How do *you* know?' enquired Sally.

'Because everyone was very keen to tell me when I flew back to Adelana. You met him four days ago——'

'And that was enough.' Sally turned away and put the kettle on. She felt something wrench at her shoulder, and was pulled round. 'Don't turn away from me!' Talitha snapped. 'He's married you in a fit of pique, that's all. The marriage can be annulled—you'll get a good price for your little game—and then you can go back home to London.'

It seemed as if Luke was a spectator. Sally thought: he's watching, he's listening—and he doesn't care. She brushed the shoulder of her housecoat where Talitha had touched, then she sighed, ever so gently.

'You're making a spectacle of yourself,' she said quietly. 'I don't know who you're trying to impress, but it's not doing much for me. Why don't you go back to Australia, or wherever it is you were, and do your act there? The Aussies like big tough women . . .'

She thought she heard a faint snort, but it might have been her imagination.

'Don't talk clever-clever, English miss!' Talitha snapped. Two pink spots burned on her exquisite cheeks, and her eyes sparked with temper. 'I can sort you out in no time at all, if I choose, but you're not worth it. Luke and I belong to each other—have for three years—and I do mean *belong*. One night in the hay with a snooty English rose is hardly going to make him want to give up all I can offer him.'

'Then why didn't he marry you?' Sally enquired, eyes wide with innocence.

'Because *I* didn't choose . . .'

'Or weren't asked?' Sally laughed merrily. 'Excuse me, the water's boiling.' And she poured it into the coffee percolator with a steady hand.

'Damn you—you little bitch——' The attack took her by surprise. Sally felt a blow on her cheek and gasped. Before she could retaliate, Luke had swung Talitha away from her, holding her by the shoulders. 'Okay,' he said. 'That's enough.'

'Let her go,' Sally cut in. 'I can cope. I don't need help. And she doesn't bother me.' Her cheek stung, but she didn't touch it. She waited, breathing hard, and watched the woman struggling in Luke's grasp. How could he have had her for his mistress? Perhaps he was a masochist, not a sadist at all. Perhaps he enjoyed suffering. Talitha, as if realising she had gone too far, relaxed slightly.

Then Sally saw the transformation in her, and her question was answered. Talitha's face softened, the hard anger vanished, and her mouth curved sensually.

'Darling,' she breathed, 'oh, darling, forgive me, I've been such a silly girl losing my temper like that, but it's only because I love you so.'

She's either, thought Sally bemused, the most marvellous actress that's ever been born, or she genuinely means it. The change was fantastic; it might have been a different woman altogether from the one who had come tearing in breathing fire and fury. This was a warm, feminine and utterly beautiful woman who moved slowly from Luke's restraining grasp, who turned limpid eyes on Sally, who said, with what Sally would have sworn was a sob in her voice:

'Please forgive me.' But then Sally saw the gleam in

Talitha's eyes, and she knew. She took a deep breath.

'Of course I forgive you, Talitha.' She smiled gently. 'I can hardly blame you for being so—hurt and upset.' Two can play at your little game, she thought. On Luke's face was something approaching bewilderment. Just wait, thought Sally. 'Sit down. Let's talk it over like adults, shall we? You'll have a drink? Are you hungry?'

'Just orange juice, that will be fine.' Talitha sat down, every movement graceful, and lowered her eyes. Her lip quivered. Any minute now, Sally thought coolly, she'll get out a handkerchief. Which was precisely what she did a moment later. Gently she dabbed her eyes, and Sally saw Luke watching her. There was nothing on his face to give him away. He looked as hard and tough as ever. And Sally, who had just about had enough of everything, poured out two coffees and handed one to Luke. Then she poured a glassful of orange juice out, held it up, said: 'Will this be enough for you, Talitha?'

The other woman looked up. The tears looked genuine enough, but probably a crocodile's did as well. 'Lovely,' she breathed.

'Then enjoy it,' said Sally very sweetly. 'It should cool you down.' And walking over, she carefully tipped the full glass of juice over Talitha's beautiful head.

The shriek of fury that erupted from the furious spluttering woman would have sent a decibel counter soaring. It filled the house. As she jumped to her feet, spitting obscenities, Sally picked up her coffee and walked out of the kitchen. In the moment of silence that came as Talitha drew breath, she said to Luke:

'I'll leave you two lovebirds to talk.' She closed the door, went into the bedroom, sat on the bed, and began to drink her coffee. I enjoyed that, she thought. I really enjoyed that. And she smiled to herself.

She timed it on her watch. Twenty-two minutes precisely. Then Luke walked into the bedroom and said: 'She's gone.'

'I know. I heard the door slam. I'm going to make breakfast now.' She stood up, fastened the belt of her housecoat more securely, picked up her cup, and walked past Luke into the kitchen.

'Why did you do it?' he enquired from the doorway.

'Why did I do what?' Sally looked across from where she bent at the refrigerator.

'Pour the stuff all over her.'

Sally straightened up. She thought about it for a second. 'It appeared to be the right thing to do at the time.' She gave him a brilliant smile. 'Why? Did it make you angry?'

'No. You did it beautifully. There was a certain expertise. Do you make a habit of it?'

'No.' She shook her head. 'I can't say I do, actually. Only when I meet people like Talitha.'

'Which isn't often.'

'You could say that.' She began to hum softly to herself as she took four eggs from the basin and replaced it in the refrigerator. 'Er—you do like eggs, do you? Only I make quite a good omelette.'

'Fine.' He was watching her, so she continued her

humming, broke and separated the eggs, and began to beat the whites with a whisk from the drawer. The name of the game is coolness, she thought.

'I'd appreciate an omelette pan, if there is one. If not a frying pan will do.'

He silently opened a cupboard and handed her one. 'Thanks.' She carried on working. Nothing can hurt me any more, she thought. I've built up a little wall, and I'm immune, hurray, hurray. She mouthed the words silently as he hummed her little tune, and everything was going to be all right. Because whatever Luke did from now on, it didn't matter. And she would have sworn he sensed her mood; he didn't look puzzled. He was too shrewd for that. But he, for one, was not entirely in control of the situation.

'Please sit down, it's nearly ready,' she said a few minutes later. This was going to be the ultimate—the perfect—omelette. And it required serving at the precise moment she tipped it from the pan to warmed plate. She waited until his fork cut into its delicious fluffiness, then said in very level, very calm tones:

'I've had my first lesson—no, sorry, the first two. Perhaps you'd be good enough to warn me when the next one's coming up.' She paused to let the words sink in, smiled pleasantly at him, and added: 'I'm going to have a shower now—I need one,' and sailed out of the kitchen.

When she had showered, rubbed her hair dry, and emerged from the shower in snappy white shorts and sun-top, she felt even more confident. She didn't feel hungry after all, so she put the remaining eggs away. Of Luke—her husband—there was no sign.

She poured herself a glass of orange juice, added two lumps of ice—and giggled at a sudden thought. Then Luke walked in carrying huge yellow fruits she didn't recognise.

'Another private joke?' he asked dryly.

'Oh *no*, you can share this. I was just thinking how much more beautiful it would have been if I'd put ice in Talitha's drink. She might have had to fish the lumps out from that gorgeous blouse top.'

'You made quite a mess as it was,' he pointed out. 'Orange juice in hair is hardly the nicest sensation. She looked distinctly sticky when she eventually stormed out.'

'Did you ever love her?' She hadn't intended to ask it.

'No.'

'It's none of my business anyway.'

'You're right, it's not. But seeing that you gave her the biggest shock of her life, I feel you deserve a slight explanation of our relationship.'

'Please——' Sally smiled most charmingly, 'I can imagine. It was an—adult—understanding.'

'Something like that. You put it quite delicately. No strings on either side. Just the way we both wanted it. Only, recently, she changed, became more—possessive is the only way I can put it. And, presumably to incite me to jealousy, she announced that she was going on holiday to Australia to visit her cousin—male, of course—and I said okay, fine, but if she went our affair would be over.' He smiled reflectively. 'No one ever tells Talitha what to do—she's like you in that respect. She went, happy, confident I'd be waiting with open arms when she returned.'

'My visit could hardly have come at a more opportune moment,' she murmured, and sipped her drink.

'If you like,' he shrugged.

Sally emptied her glass, carried it to the sink and rinsed it. 'Right,' she said. She had tired of the brief conversation about Talitha. 'Hadn't you better give me orders for the day?' And she waited, with a submissive look on her face, a patient, sweet, whatever-you-say look. It didn't come easily—but I'm still learning, she thought.

His answer surprised her. 'I think enough has happened for one day. We'll go swimming. You can swim?'

'Of course.'

'Underwater?'

'Er—with snorkels?'

'No. I mean really underwater, with oxygen.'

'No. I don't think——' She shook her head.

'Scared?'

She took a deep breath. The new-found poise hadn't prepared her for this.

'I'm not sure,' she confessed.

'Then we can try. You'll enjoy it.'

'But I'm not hear to *enjoy* myself. So wouldn't it be better for me to watch you?' Point to me, she thought.

He laughed. '*Touché.* Quick on the answers too. Yes, I insist.'

'Very well. What about sharks?'

'No danger—not here anyway. Perhaps the odd basking shark, but there's little likelihood. Anyway, if it makes you feel better I'll carry some shark repellant. See anything and we'll spray—fast.'

'Then let's get going,' she smiled.

'Got a swimsuit?'

'Yes. I'll go and change.' She went out, rummaged through the drawers where she had put her clothes and pulled out the skimpy white bikini she had brought. She put it on and looked at herself in the mirror. Mmm, she thought, not bad. Barefoot she padded out and shouted: 'I'm ready!'

She saw his eyes, just for that brief moment at his first sight of her, before he could manage to hide the expression, and she turned away and walked out of the front door. There was a hidden feeling of satisfaction mingled with excitement inside her. She had seen, for just a moment, but that had been enough; a sensuous flaring of naked desire. For her, not for the woman he thought about all the other times. Just for her.

They were in a different world; a warm, dreamy slow-motion undersea world of silence and breathtaking beauty. The water was so clear that it was possible to see a long distance, and the richness of plants and fish, all colourful and exotic, like none she had ever seen before, made a heady blend to stir the senses.

They were near the shore, at a depth of ten feet or so, with the sea bottom not far below them, and movement was so easy, and the water was a silken caress against the skin. Sally twisted so that she was swimming on her back, and looked up to see the strangest, most incredible sight. It was as if there were a roof above her, but one that glinted and sparkled with a million golden flashes of light. The surface of the water, with the sun shining on it. Had anyone described it to her, she would not have believed it, but she was seeing it for herself, was seeing the kind of beauty she had never seen before, and it made her feel strangely humble—an entirely new sensation. It was like suddenly seeing the whole of her life in perspective.

She looked round for Luke, and he was a distance away, crouching on the ocean floor, examining a huge rock with plants growing from it, plants that drifted and swayed in time with his movements. Sally floated down to join him, and he pointed to a tiny crevice at the base of the rock, and a tiny crab scuttled in to hide, leaving a flurry of sand behind it. A huge fish loomed up, took one look at them, and veered away, eyes gleaming. He had said they wouldn't stay down long, as it was her first time, but she could have stayed there for ever. The world and everyone in it seemed tremendously far away and unimportant.

Luke pointed upwards, then made the gesture that meant—slowly, and Sally gave him the thumbs up sign. He had said, before they walked into the water, that the ascent to the surface must always be slow and unhurried so that their bodies could adjust to the pressure, so that there would be no danger.

Now, gently, they drifted upwards, paused, waited, then upwards again, and reached the surface, bursting out of the sea in a final shoosh of sound.

A leisurely swim, until their feet touched sand, then the walk in, and how weary Sally's limbs were now! It was an effort to move. She collapsed on to the beach, and began unstrapping her oxygen belt.

'Oh, that was marvellous!' She looked up at him, laughing, and Luke sat down beside her. Even he had a more calm look about him. Perhaps, she thought, it changes you, going in there. I wonder what it could do for Talitha? And she laughed.

Before he could ask, she told him, 'I was laughing— I was wondering what effect that little trip would have on our recent visitor. Has she ever done any?'

'Not her! Why?'

'Because——' she shrugged. 'Oh, I don't know, it's difficult to put into words—it's like a different world out there, like nothing I could ever have imagined. So peaceful, so utterly calm—and everything seems unimportant.'

'You felt it too, did you? I was curious. I wondered——'

'Is that why you took me? Is it part of the "lessons"?'

He laughed. 'Perhaps.' The wide mouth twisted, became cynical. 'You're not quite as hard as I thought. If you can feel that, maybe there's hope for you yet.'

He had spoiled it. In those few words ... Sally smiled. 'How kind you are,' she breathed. 'How terribly kind!'

He tipped her chin, making her face him, and saw the anger in her eyes. 'Don't be sarcastic,' he said. 'It doesn't become you—and I don't like it.'

'Good,' she retorted. 'I must remember that. Hard? *Hard! You* can talk about me being hard? My God, what do you think *you* are? If I'm hard, you're pure granite!' She pushed his hand away, and her breathing was quick and shallow. She felt quite dizzy all of a sudden, and was alarmed. She wanted to get up and walk away from him, back to the house, but her legs were heavy, and it was too much effort to try and move yet.

'Don't start a fight,' he said, but he didn't look even mildly angry, more amused. 'You won't win.'

'I couldn't at the moment,' she shot back. 'So you're *quite* safe.'

'I know. You're as weak as a kitten. That's how it gets you—the first time. Until you're used to it.'

She took a deep breath. Calm, calm, she told herself. The new you, the one that doesn't care about anything, remember? Don't let that go away. She forced herself to speak very casually. 'So that's why we didn't stay out too long? I see.'

'That's it.' He was watching her, speculatively, as if he could read her mind—as if he could see her innermost thoughts. And that Sally wasn't going to have. She lay back.

'I think I'll lie and sunbathe for a while,' she said, closing her eyes. 'With your permission, of course.'

'No. It's lunch-time. I'm hungry. You can get me some food.'

'Again? Good heavens, do you spend all your time eating?'

'I warned you. Watch that tongue of yours. You can prepare a salad from the mangoes I picked.'

So that was what the fruit had been. 'Sorry, oh master,' she said sweetly. 'I'll try and remember.' She opened her eyes and looked hard at him. 'Mango salad. Mmm, sounds scrumptious. And then what?'

'Steak. You can manage to grill that, I take it?'

'Possibly. I dare say you'll take yours very rare.'

'No. I like mine well done, as a matter of fact.'

'Oh dear, I must remember to make a note of all these little things. It will save me keep asking you. Anything else I should know?'

'That's enough for now. Don't worry, I'll let you know if you do anything wrong.'

'I'm sure you will.' Her eyes widened. 'Oh yes, I'm quite sure you'll be good at *that*.' Thank goodness the dizzy sensation was passing, and she was fast regaining her strength.

'Then let's move,' he said.

'In a minute.' She wasn't quite sure if she could stand. She hadn't eaten anything, she suddenly remembered that. It was little wonder she still felt weak. 'When I'm ready to move.' She smiled languorously.

'Now!'

'No!'

Their eyes met and clashed in a silent battle of wills, and Sally was determined not to look away first. Then Luke caught her wrist.

'Damn you!' she exclaimed. 'Don't *touch* me!' She tried to jerk her hand free, but the grip was of steel.

'Touch you? I'll touch you whenever I want. You're my wife, remember?'

'I can't forget it!' Nor could she forget that softly murmured name; she wouldn't ever be able to forget *that*. 'And *my* name's Sally.'

'What's that supposed to mean?' His grip tightened

imperceptibly, and suddenly she was frightened of
him.

'Nothing. Let me go—I'll get up——'

'Not until you tell me——'

'Ouch! You're hurting!'

'I'll hurt you more before I've finished, you
little——'

She reached up her free hand and hit him hard, then
tried to twist herself free of him, stopping his words.
'Then hurt me! Go on—hit me if that's what you
want, and get it over with!' A sob was wrenched from
her as she struggled vainly to escape, then she went
limp, exhausted. It was all going wrong again. She
must stop, she must remember all the things she had
told herself—she must, or she would go mad.

'I won't hit you,' he grated, and his weight came
down on her. 'I'd like to beat you, but I wouldn't.
You are infuriating, and maddening, and you deserve
a damned good hiding.'

'Then why don't you?' His face was only inches
away from hers. 'Anything is preferable to ...' She
turned her face sideways, away from him.

'To what?' His voice had gone harsher, harder.
'Look at me when you talk to me. Preferable to
what?'

'I should think you know already,' she breathed, and
slowly turned to face him again. 'You're heavy—
please, I——'

'But I want you to tell me.' His eyes had darkened.
She saw in them what she had seen before, and now
she could not look away. She moistened her lips. There

was no strength in her, none at all. 'Than making love,' she managed to whisper.

'And who invited it?' His voice was strangely husky. 'Did I force you?'

'No, I—it was a mistake—I didn't mean ...'

She moaned softly as his lips came down on hers in a long, lingering kiss of fire. Then he whispered in her ear: 'Then let there be no mistake this time, my dear wife,' and his lips found her cheek, brushed across to her mouth, and she was lost.

'No—I——' Her protest grew fainter. Desperately, in her mind, she tried to recall what it was that had so upset her before, but she was drowning, her senses reeling helplessly, whole body on fire with treacherous sweet longing that could not be refused.

The water, lapping around their feet and legs, pulsed in a gentle rhythm against the sands, and somewhere in the distance a gull cried harshly, but they neither of them heard anything.

# CHAPTER SEVEN

SALLY prepared the lunch, ate a small piece of steak, then pushed her plate away and stood up.

Luke paused in the act of cutting his steak, and looked up at her and asked: 'Where are you going?'

'To lie down. I don't feel well.' She didn't wait to see if he would answer her; she didn't look at him, she simply walked out of the room, into the bedroom, and lay down on the bed. She had told him the simple truth—she felt wretched. And she knew why. A deep shame filled her, a revulsion that made her head and body ache. She was hardly able to think coherently, she was desperately tired, longing for nothing more than sleep and oblivion. But that was denied her. She couldn't even relax, let alone rest. She lay there unmoving, while the memories rushed back to taunt her, and she opened her eyes—and saw Luke standing in the doorway watching her.

She turned her head away. 'Leave me alone, please,' she whispered.

'What's the matter with you?' But he knew. He knew very well, and if he had come to mock her she would have been unable to bear it.

'My head aches.' That at least was quite true.

'Then I'll get you something. Why didn't you say?'

'It doesn't matter. It'll pass.'

But he had already gone out, and she waited. 'Here, drink this.' He handed her a glass of water and two pills, waited until she had swallowed them, and took the half empty glass back. 'Shall I draw the blinds?'

'Yes. Please.'

'Then I'll leave you. But you must eat later. You've had nothing today, have you?' He pulled down the blinds and secured them.

'No.' Only you, she thought, and that was more than enough.

'Shout me if you want me.' He held the door. Want you? Want *you*? she thought hysterically. Oh God, I don't want you at all, ever again. I wish you'd just go away.

'I will,' she answered softly.

He went out and closed the door, and she was left alone again. The silence washed round her; gradually she felt herself relaxing, and even more gradually, sleep came to her at last.

When she awoke she was not aware of the time, or how long she had slept. She had taken her watch off before swimming, and it was too much trouble to get up and look at it. She felt better, and she lay there, and the thoughts she had managed to repress before came flooding back. Now, alone, feeling physically stronger, she was able to think clearly, and to admit to herself something she had known since last evening. She had read about it happening, and she had never believed it, simply because, in her cynical smart world, it didn't happen. People had affairs, got married, divorced, formed shallow temporary liaisons and told the world

that they loved each other, and it was for keeps . . . and
nothing ever lasted, because none of them knew what
love was. Nor had Sally. Until now. Until, the previous
evening, she had known the growing awareness after
Luke's first shattering lovemaking, but had denied it
to herself.

But then, on the beach, hours previously, when he
had taken complete command, and had made love to
her savagely, deliciously, rapturously—then she had
known completely. And he, who had married her only
for his own personal revenge, would never love anybody. He hadn't loved Talitha, he disliked Sally in-
tensely. That was made quite clear. She moved, in an
anguish of unhappiness that swept over her, and knew
that he had already succeeded in what he had set out
to do. He would use her, that was all. The only woman
he had ever loved was dead, and beyond that nothing
mattered to him. He was a man of strong physical
needs, and he would satisfy them, whether with
Talitha, Sally—or some other woman. It didn't matter.
For the first time, Sally actually felt sorry for his ex-
mistress. They had a lot in common, did Talitha but
know it. She moved her head restlessly in anguish.
That it should have happened like this! To discover
her innermost feelings, to know what it was to be a
complete woman—with a man whose only emotions
were gone for ever—was shattering. She knew that
she must leave him as soon as possible, if she was to
retain any shreds of dignity or self-respect.

The door clicked, and she stiffened. Then it opened,
very quietly, and Sally felt warmth creeping over her.
Don't let him see, she thought desperately. Don't let

him ever guess. That would be the final shame of all.

'You're awake?' asked Luke.

'Yes. What time is it?'

'Nearly six. It will be dark very shortly. Are you better?'

'Yes. I'll get up now.'

'I've made a meal,' he told her. 'It's ready. You must eat.'

'I will. I'm hungry—at least I think I am.' He walked over and sat on the bed, and she caught her breath, frightened that she might cry out.

'I'm not going to touch you,' he said softly. Was it so obvious?

'I—I didn't think you were.'

'You flinched. Do I frighten you so?'

'Yes. But then that's what you want, isn't it?'

'I'm not sure. You're not as tough as I thought you were.'

She looked at him, drinking in his features, knowing she would have to remember that face when she went away, needing to take it all in now, so that she would be able to see it at will. Because that will be all I will have, she thought. How ironic! Are Laura's features etched on his brain for ever so that he sees only her when he's . . .

'Why do you look at me like that?' I must be more careful, she thought. He's too clever by far.

'Can't I look?' She managed a certain flippancy.

'Of course.'

She closed her eyes. 'It's getting cooler now. I'll change and then I'll come out.'

He stood up. 'Very well.' The next moment she was

alone. She let out her breath in a long shuddering sigh. Where's this wall I built about myself? she thought, as she stood up and began to unfasten her bikini top. Because I need it now, more than ever. She put on a long flowing kaftan in thin cotton, brushed her hair, and went out to the kitchen.

The table was laid, and Luke was standing with his back to her at the cooker.

'Coffee's nearly ready,' he said. 'Sit down. I made a chicken curry—not too hot, but it'll do you good.'

It won't cure me, she thought, I wonder what will. He produced two plates from under the grill and put them on the table. Then he sat down opposite her. Sally looked at the steaming plateful of rice and chicken and rich curry gravy, then began to eat.

Later that evening, when it was dark, she said: 'I'd like to go out for a walk alone. Is it safe?'

Luke looked up from the book he was reading. They were both in the living room of the cottage, and Sally had been leafing through an old magazine, and some hours had passed since they had eaten. She sensed a strangeness about him, and she felt uneasy. She didn't understand what it was, only that there was a certain tension within him, which in its turn affected her.

'Perfectly safe. There are no snakes, but there are certain varieties of insect life that can prove irritating. There's some repellant in the bathroom. I suggest you spray yourself with it before you go.'

She put down the magazine and went out, and several minutes later was walking along the sand, letting her eyes become accustomed to the darkness. The

boom of distant breakers and the much nearer hum of
the insects were the only sounds to be heard. The sky
was a canopy of black velvet studded with brilliant
diamonds. Sally breathed deeply of the scented air. She
was alone, and it no longer bothered her; in fact she
found it attractive. She could walk as fast or as slowly
as she pleased; she could walk as far as she wanted, or
sit down and watch the white foam shushing against
the sand. And she had no need to talk, or even to think.
Time enough for that tomorrow, when she would try
and persuade Luke to take her back to Adelana.

The plans were already forming in her mind. She
would see her uncle and Rosa on her return, and she
would tell Rosa everything about the bizarre marriage
pact—and persuade her to leave the island and seek
treatment for her husband. Rosa would understand,
and as her first and only concern was Alistair's welfare,
she would co-operate.

Once they were gone Sally would escape too. Because
the burden of being married to Luke was more than
she could bear. He might possibly take the villa from
them, but they would have the money. She sat down
on the sand as that thought came to her. Was it dis-
honest? Possibly, yet she had married Luke—and
that had been the only condition for the handing over
of the money. Nothing had been said about afterwards. Legally then, no, but morally—Sally shrugged.
Where would Luke stand—morally—with his plans
for revenge? He was worse than anyone she had ever
known; his behaviour was despicable.

And yet I love him, she thought, as she sat on the
sand, hugging her knees. I can't get him out of my

mind, when I know how he feels about me—and that his only emotion for me is contempt. She closed her eyes. With the ring that she would leave him would be a note, and in it she would tell him that he had succeeded in his plan for revenge. And the very fact of her being able to write it should be enough proof of the truth. She sighed. What a mess it all was! The only good thing to come out of it would be that Uncle Alistair would have benefited. But that was enough, more than enough.

She wondered how Rosa would react to what she was going to hear. She would soon know. And then— escape. Back to England, perhaps a few weeks away from London—for she wasn't due back for six weeks, and they would all wonder, and speculate why. Not that she cared any more, but a holiday would do her good. And this was supposed to be a holiday, she thought. There's a laugh! Only she didn't feel like laughing; she felt more like crying.

It was time to go back. And if Luke made love to her again, tonight or ever, she would keep some part of her mind detached from it all, out of the simple desire for self-protection. She got to her feet, dusted the sand from her dress, and set off walking back.

He didn't make any attempt to even touch her. Sally lay wide awake, listening to his steady breathing, and knew he was asleep. He had hardly spoken when she returned to the cottage, had merely said: 'I'm going to have a shower and go to bed,' and had gone. He had been reading when she went in, and hadn't even looked up. The atmosphere hadn't changed. There was uneasiness in the air, yet she couldn't understand why, and when at last she knew she wouldn't get to sleep she quietly slipped out to the kitchen and mixed a drink of fruit juice and sat there sipping it, reading the magazine. Nothing registered. Five minutes after she put it down, she had forgotten what she had read. She got into bed and lay beside him, and her mind was in a turmoil.

'We're going back to Adelana today,' he said, as Sally prepared the toast for his breakfast the following morning. She nearly dropped the plate she was holding. How could he have known?

'I see. When?'

'After lunch.'

'I'll get packed.'

'Don't you want to know why we're going?'

'You have your reasons.' She passed him the plate with the toast on. 'I have no right to ask.'

'I have work to do, that's all.' He began to eat, and she turned away to pour out his coffee—it wasn't all, she knew that. Something about him was different. He was harder, remote, like the stranger she had first known. And her only consoling thought was—it won't be for long. Not much longer.

The morning passed, and Sally cleaned the kitchen thoroughly and packed her case, and prepared a light lunch for them both, but she felt nothing. Every action was mechanical, and when Luke spoke, she answered. It was as though something had died inside her. But she thought fiercely—you can't hurt me any more, I know that now. She needed that knowledge to keep her going. She counted the hours until she would be able to talk to Rosa, and it wouldn't be long, not long.

When they walked to the plane, and when they were taking off, she looked at the island that had no name, and thought: I shall never come here again. I shan't even be able to find it on a map—and it will be as though it had never existed, as though none of this had ever happened. And it seemed to her appropriate that the place should be nameless.

'Fasten your seat belt, Sally, we're off.'

'Right. Fastened.'

They gathered speed, then the sensation of lifting, of lightness, and she turned once to look, to see the island receding for the last time, and then looked forward. Everything was blurred, but she had only to blink a few times and her eyes were back to normal. End of honeymoon, and soon the end of marriage, she thought wryly.

A car was waiting for them, with the same driver, and they were whisked away from the airstrip and soon climbing a twisting road into the hills. I don't even know where we're going to live, Sally thought. Nor if there are servants, and how many. I know nothing, and yet I'm returning from honeymoon with my husband, who has suddenly become more of a stranger than he was the first time I saw him. She looked at him.

He sat beside her, remote, hawklike profile, that strong chin, that mouth ... Big, lean—and dangerous. So why hadn't she trusted her instinct, kept strictly out of his way? Because I'm a fool, she thought.

'May I telephone my uncle and aunt when we reach the—your—house?' she asked.

'Of course.' He spared her only a brief glance.

'Thank you.' And that was the end of their conversation. Until they reached the gates of a house, and the car went up the drive, and she saw and exclaimed:

'How beautiful!' She didn't know what she had expected. Perhaps, in the back of her mind, had been pictures of an opulent mansion—but this was a large white house. Beautiful, yes, but only in its simplicity and cleanness of lines, the sheer magnificence being in the rich gardens surrounding it, cascading flowers, shrubs and trees, and over all, an atmosphere of calm and tranquillity. It was not the place Sally would have pictured, for him. And yet she did not know him at all, so she could hardly be surprised.

'My housekeeper will have prepared our dinner,' he said, as the car drew to a halt on the red gravel sweep of drive at the front. 'You'll meet her soon.'

She followed him into a cool hall with mirrored walls and white-tiled floor, and looked around her. 'Ah, there you are, Wilma. Sally, this is Wilma, who looks after me—Wilma, Sally—my wife.'

The tall coloured woman had been waiting, apparently, and stepped forward. She was perhaps sixty, her hair white, her face dignified and aloof. Then she smiled, and subtly, all was changed.

'How do you do, Mrs Vilis,' she said. There was warmth in her voice.

'How do you do.' Sally sensed an ally, yet did not know why.

'I'll show you up to your room. Mr Vilis, there are

several messages for you, on the pad by the telephone.'

'I'll attend to them now. Yes, show Sally around. I'll not be long.'

Sally followed the woman up curving stairs, the delicate wrought iron banisters as fragile-looking as spiders' webs, and on to a wide landing with several doors leading off. The housekeeper opened one, and ushered Sally in.

'Anything you want, Mrs Vilis—anything—you call me. I'll come!' She smiled, teeth white in her dusky face. 'I never thought the day would come when I'd welcome a bride again, and you've made my day complete.' She stopped. 'I'm sorry, ma'am. That was impertinent.'

'No, it wasn't,' answered Sally quietly. 'You—were here when Mr Vilis was married before?'

The woman's face softened. It seemed to Sally that she breathed a sigh of relief. 'You know? Thank the lord! I spoke without thinking. But I love Mr Vilis like he was a son—and he's been too long alone.'

Alone? It seemed a strange thing to say, having met Talitha, and Sally echoed the word. 'Alone? But——'

Very quietly, Wilma closed the door. 'Lonely—perhaps that's a wiser word.'

Sally had to know. Just one question, that was all. And there was time. 'Wilma, tell me—what was Laura, Mrs Vilis, like? Was she beautiful?'

'Oh yes, she was. She was the loveliest woman I ever saw——' She stopped, and her eyes were very gentle on Sally, who caught her breath, because something told her what was to come next, and she wasn't sure if she wanted to hear. 'Why, she looked a lot like you,

Mrs Vilis. I thought it the minute I set eyes on you——'

'No!' The word was wrenched from Sally. 'Don't—please don't say that!'

'I'm sorry, ma'am. I'd better go.' Wilma's face showed her distress, and she half turned. Sally caught her arm.

'Don't go. Forgive me—that was a stupid thing for me to say. I—*knew* you were going to say it, and it was a shock to hear it, that's all.' She smiled. 'It's all right, Wilma. That was strictly between us—feminine curiosity, I suppose. I won't mention it again. I'm tired after travelling and everything—and more than a little hungry.'

'The meal's ready when you are, then I'll unpack for you. There's a bell at the side of the bed. Ring it if you need anything.' She paused and shook her head. 'I guess I got a surprise when I saw you at last, that's all, even though my husband had told me.'

'Your husband?' Sally frowned, puzzled.

'Mr Vilis's chauffeur. He took you to the airstrip and just brought you back. He said, when he returned after taking you just after the wedding, "Why, Wilma," he said, "she ain't half like the first Mrs Vilis"—and now I know what he means.' She opened the door. Just as she went out, she paused. 'I know you'll make him very happy.' Then she had gone.

Sally was left standing in the centre of the large bedroom. She had had enough surprises—too many. But this was subtly different, one she could not have imagined. Could there be a third reason why Luke had married her? She put her hand to her mouth, fighting self-control before he returned. Oh God, it could explain so much, so very much. She had wondered what Laura had looked like, and now she knew. The name seemed to echo mockingly round the room as if her ghost were there watching. There was something else she had to know. She pressed the bell by the bed, not caring if Luke were to come in. If he did, she would ask the housekeeper some perfectly innocuous question. She waited in a fever of impatience and called: 'Come in,' as the tap came at the door, and Wilma opened it.

'One thing I must know. Did—they live here, in this house?'

Wilma shook her head. 'Why, no, ma'am. We were in another place altogether. Not here. It was many years ago.'

'How many?'

'At least twelve. Mr Vilis was in his early twenties— are you all right, Mrs Vilis?'

'Yes, I'm fine.' Sally sat down on the bed. 'I'm sorry, but I had to know. Silly of me.'

There was a look of infinite compassion on the other woman's face. 'It's not silly at all. It's the most natural question in the world. Shall I bring you a drink? A drop of brandy—you're quite white.' She paused. 'And he could be a while—there were quite a few messages for him. He'll be on that telephone for ages if I know him.'

'Is there more than one telephone? I don't mean extension, I mean a separate line that I can use?'

'Why, surely, that one beside the bed. The one he's on is a private one only he uses.'

'Good. I'll have the drink later. I have to phone my uncle. He lives here on Adelana.'

'That'll be Mr Herrick, won't it?' Wilma nodded. 'A very nice gentleman. I'll go down and leave you in peace.' And she went out.

Sally dialled her uncle's number, and Rosa answered. 'Hello, Rosa? It's me—Sally.'

'Hello. Where are you?'

'We're back at Luke's house. Rosa, can I come over tomorrow?—I have to collect some things—and I'd like to talk to you.'

Rosa's voice was cool, non-committal. 'To me—or to Alistair?'

Sally took a deep breath. 'To you—in private if possible.'

'Is there—something wrong?'

That would be an understatement of majestic proportions. Sally couldn't be sure if any of her conversation was overheard, and her reply was as casual as Rosa's question.

'Heavens, no! I'd just like a chat, that's all.'

'Then I'll be in. Alistair has a rest after lunch——'

'Yes, I understand. I'll see you then. Goodbye.'

'All right. Did you enjoy your honeymoon?'

'It was lovely,' Sally told her.

'Fine. See you tomorrow. Goodbye, Sally.' The telephone was replaced with a firm click.

Tomorrow. Tomorrow, she would start everything rolling. A quotation from a book came into Sally's head. Tomorrow is the first day of the rest of your life. That seemed to sum it up quite accurately. She stood up and walked to the window to look out at the gardens. After tomorrow . . .

She watched Luke with new eyes at dinner. So I look like Laura, do I, she thought. That explains much I had already guessed. She was calm, almost icily under control, and her poise never faltered even when Wilma came in as they were eating the dessert to say that Luke was wanted on the telephone.

He looked up and frowned. 'Who is it?'

Wilma glanced at Sally, then back again to Luke. 'Miss Gervaise,' she said, very reluctantly. 'Shall I say you're engaged?'

He pushed his chair back, and it scraped on the tiled floor. 'No, I'll take it. Excuse me, Sally.'

'Certainly.' She spooned up the delicious mousse. 'You're a wonderful cook, Wilma. I must come and see you in action some time.' Then, seeing the housekeeper's face: 'It's all right, I've met Miss Gervaise. You don't need to look so worried.'

Wilma visibly relaxed. 'Oh, thank the lord!' Then, startled:. 'You've *met* her?'

Sally laughed. 'We had an—encounter, yes. She flew by helicopter to where we were honeymooning.'

'Oh! My lord!' Wilma put her hand to her mouth, eyes wide.

'Would it upset you to know that I poured a glass of orange juice over her head——?' Sally had hardly finished before Wilma burst out laughing, her face creasing in sheer enjoyment. She wiped her eyes on her apron, shoulders shaking.

'Oh, Mrs Vilis, you didn't? *Did* you?'

'Mmm, I did, and you know something? I enjoyed it.'

Wilma gave a sigh of relief. 'Then you don't like her either?'

'You could say that.' Sally frowned. 'I wonder what she wants?'

'It's none of my business, ma'am—but I'll tell you anyway—be careful of her. She could make a bad enemy.'

'You don't need to tell me,' Sally answered quietly. But she didn't add that it didn't matter. Talitha would soon have no competition at all—and strangely, at that thought, Sally felt sorry for Wilma. Because Luke and his ex-mistress might just get together again. And there was nothing she, Sally, could say to warn her. She smiled at the housekeeper. The least she could do was to tell Luke, in the note she would leave when she went, that Wilma respected him greatly but disliked Talitha. She was aware of Luke's high regard for his housekeeper, from the way he spoke to her. It would help, she knew that. And it could do no harm. Sally instinctively liked and trusted the older woman. If only everything were different . . .

'Well, that was delicious.' She pushed her plate aside. 'Luke will be back in a minute. He'd better not catch us talking about you-know-who, had he?'

Wilma smiled a conspiratorial smile. 'No, that would never do. But I'm glad you know, ma'am. It makes things easier for me. If she calls—when Mr Vilis is out—shall I say you're out too?'

Sally shook her head. 'No. She doesn't frighten me. Don't worry.'

'As long as you're sure——' The other woman looked doubtful.

'I am.' Sally's voice was very firm.

The door opened, and Luke came in. One look at his face was enough. Wilma silently collected the empty plates, and went out, while Sally waited for she knew not what. The silence grew, and became oppressive. There was a smouldering anger about him, and when she could stand the atmosphere no longer, Sally stood up.

'Excuse me, I'm going up to——'

'Wait.' His voice was harsher than she had ever known it. 'If Talitha phones, you're to put the phone down. If she calls when I'm not here, you're not to see her.'

In the light of her conversation with Wilma, his words had the oddest effect. Sally stood by her chair and looked at him. 'Is that an order?' she asked quietly.

'Yes.'

'Then may I ask why? You don't think she'd upset me, do you—and would you care anyway?' Everything was quite calm. As far as Sally was concerned, they might have been discussing some mundane household matter. His anger was real and tangible, but strangely, now, the effect on her only served to heighten her own self-control.

He looked up, and she was almost rocked on her feet by what she saw in his eyes. 'Yes, I think she would upset you. I think she would try to do more. I think —no, I'm certain—that she would try to harm you.'

Sally sat down, very slowly. 'You're trying to tell me

she'd——' she stopped. How could you say 'try and kill me?' It was too bizarre to be real.

'She's dangerous. She could do anything——'

'She's jealous, and she's hurt, and I wouldn't put it past her to try and scratch my eyes out—but I'm as strong as she is, so——'

'She's infinitely more cunning than you. I've known her true nature for a while, but I ignored it. Now I can't. I'll instruct Wilma and John—her husband—that she's not to be allowed here. And you're not to go out alone. And that's an order, and you will obey.'

'Why should you care?' Sally wasn't frightened. She didn't understand why herself. She should have been, but it didn't seem to matter. And if she could tell him now what was going to happen—that she wouldn't be here to be harmed—but she couldn't—it wouldn't matter anyway ...

'I care for life.'

'That's no answer,' she retorted. 'Say it. Do you honestly think she wants to kill me or something?'

'Yes.'

'My God!' Sally clutched the table. 'You couldn't have planned this in your little scheme, could you? I mean, I'm to be humiliated, fine, and taught a lesson—but kept alive. Well, thank you, husband mine, you've restored my faith in human nature.' She stood up. 'All right, I'll stay in, I won't go out alone. I think you've exaggerated the situation—perhaps for reasons of your own—but I'll go along with it because I don't really have any choice.'

Luke stood as well. 'Believe me, I didn't plan *this*. And I'm not exaggerating, I mean every word I've said.' He paused. 'And I'll tell you something else. You've got more guts than I thought.' He looked deep into her eyes. 'I honestly think you mean what you say. You're not frightened of her, are you?' Silence filled the room as he waited for her answer.

'No, I'm not. It's not particularly a question of courage. It's a question of my own self-respect. Perhaps I've learned a few things from you already, who knows?' And she turned and walked out of the room, head held high.

# CHAPTER EIGHT

Rosa sat opposite Sally, and her face showed her feelings. She was stunned. Sally had told her everything, sparing no details of Luke's reasons for marriage, and of everything that had happened since. Everything except the most intimate details, that was, and they had no bearing on anything else. And Rosa had listened without saying a word, sceptical at the beginning, her face gradually changing with each twist and turn of the tale.

She took a deep breath. 'I need a drink.' She emptied the glass of wine beside her. 'My God, Sally—every word you've said has been true, hasn't it?'

'Yes. Could I have made it up?'

'No.' Rosa shook her head. 'And you did it for Alistair?'

'Yes.' Then Sally smiled. 'Please—don't give me credit for something I'm not. I'm not noble and unselfish. I never have been, and no one changes overnight. But Uncle Alistair has always meant a great deal to me, more than you know, and somehow,' she shrugged lightly, 'it seemed the only thing to do. I had to tell someone—and you're the only one. I know you don't like me. I don't really blame you. I'm beginning to wonder if I ever liked myself. And if it's any help,

I've changed somewhat.' She pulled a little face. 'Maybe it's for the better, who knows? Only time will tell.'

Rosa's face softened. 'You have changed. You're—gentler. Does that sound an odd word to use? I mean it, though. I felt it when you came in. You are different. You even look different. Oh, Sally, what are we to do?'

'I've just told you. Persuade Uncle Alistair to go abroad—anywhere he can see the top specialists. Take your money with you—you'll have that whatever happens. I've wrestled with my conscience over this, and I know it's all right. So, if you never get to move back into the villa, that won't be too shattering, will it?'

'Of course not. This place is enough—but you, Sally—you've ruined your life—for us.'

'Not ruined—battered slightly. Temporarily. I'll live,' Sally laughed. 'Oh, it's such a relief to get it all off my chest. You can't imagine how much better I feel already. Yes, I will have another drop of wine if I may,' this as Rosa held up the decanter. 'Thanks.'

'I'll start phoning right away,' Rosa decided. 'I'll have to do it when Alistair is resting—or out—but I'll do it. I've a lot of friends in London—we'll have somewhere to stay, and we'll have the money for the very best treatment—oh, Sally, you don't know what you've done! I love Alistair so much, we'll find a way, we'll find someone who can help him——' Her eyes glowed. 'I was so hard on you when you came—can you forgive me?'

'Yes.' Sally raised her glass. 'Cheers. I even—reluctantly, I admit—admired you for your stand—and you had good reason, after all. I wasn't very nice, was

I?' she added reflectively. 'I've been a selfish, spoilt little bitch all my life.' She laughed. 'And I wouldn't have admitted *that* a week ago! I thought I was perfect.'

Rosa shook her head. 'You're so different now. It's like talking to another woman altogether.'

'Good. Then let's leave it at that, shall we? You'll let me know when you're leaving, so that I can——' Sally's voice tailed away.

'Of course.' Rosa's voice was warm.

Sally looked at her watch. 'I'd better go.' There was something she hadn't yet told her aunt—about Talitha. 'Luke is having problems with his ex-mistress.'

'Talitha Gervaise?' Rosa pulled a face. 'Her!'

'She'd like to kill me.'

'My *God*! Sally——'

'It's all right, Rosa, I'm used to the idea now. She phoned last night. Luke didn't tell me exactly what she said, but he's concerned enough to forbid me out alone—funny when you think about it, isn't it? I mean—*him* being worried about *me*.'

'It's not funny at all.' Rosa's eyes were wide with horror. 'Can't he *do* anything?'

'Have her locked up, you mean?' Sally smiled. 'I doubt it. It won't be for long anyway—although he doesn't know that. I'll soon be gone from here, and he's welcome to her again.'

'But aren't you scared?' asked Rosa.

'No. I'm surprising myself—but I'm not. If anyone had told me that weeks ago, I'd have been terrified, but it just doesn't seem important.'

'Be careful, Sally,' urged Rosa. 'She's bad. Please don't be too casual about it.'

'I won't. Of course I won't. But I don't know—I just feel indifferent to the whole thing, as if—as if——' Sally stopped. She couldn't put it into words.

'As if——?' Rosa prompted gently.

Sally looked at her. 'I don't know—that's the odd thing. As if I'm remote from the whole thing.' She pinched herself. 'See? I'm not dreaming. I'm real, and I'm here. It's just as though I know she can't harm me.'

'I hope you're right,' said Rosa uneasily.

'I'd better telephone,' Sally decided. 'Luke said I was to phone the house when I wanted to leave, and John would come and pick me up. May I?'

'Of course.'

She telephoned, and they waited, and spoke of Alistair, and of all the things that might be done for him, and then the ring came at the door. Rosa hugged Sally impulsively. 'Thank you for everything,' she whispered. 'And—I'm glad you're my niece!'

'And I couldn't wish for a nicer aunt.' Laughing, almost crying, they walked towards the hall, said their final goodbyes, after promising to keep in touch, and opened the door, to see, not John, but Luke.

'Oh!' Astonishment showed on Sally's face. 'Luke!'

'Yes, it's me. Hello, Rosa. How are you?'

'Fine, thanks, Luke. I was telling Sally how well she looked.' There was nothing in Rosa's manner to give anything away. 'Will you come in for a drink?'

'Not now, thanks. Perhaps another time. You'll come round for dinner in a day or so?'

'That would be lovely.' Rosa smiled a little smile at Sally.

'I'll let Sally fix it up, then. Goodbye.'

They got in the car, waved their farewells, and set off down the drive. Sally sat quite calmly, waiting for Luke to either tell her why he had come instead of John, or not, as he chose. She felt absurdly happy now that she had unburdened herself to Rosa, and beside that, anything else was mere trivia.

She looked out of the window at the passing scenery. It was all quite beautiful. Everything was lovely, in fact. All going to plan, and soon she wouldn't be here any more. And nothing was going to go wrong. Nothing . . .

They went up the drive slowly towards the house, and Luke stopped the car, and said: 'If you get out now, I'll put the car away.'

Sally obediently got out of the car, quite happy to do exactly as she was told, because it didn't matter, and Luke started up the limousine in preparation for driving away. Then Sally heard a faint noise, growing rapidly louder and louder, and saw a red sports car coming up the drive towards her.

She was standing by the steps, and still she didn't realise. Her only thought was: What a fast driver— then Luke was out of the car, and running towards her shouting what sounded like: 'Move, Sally, for God's sake——!' only she couldn't hear it properly above the roar of the engine—and then, too late, she knew. As Luke flung her bodily up the steps, there was a screech of brakes, mingling with her own screams, then Luke was falling, falling to the ground in a sickening slow motion, and the red car swerved and vanished in a roar round the the side of the house.

It was a nightmare, one of those where you can only move your limbs incredibly slowly, and something nameless is pursuing you—and you can't breathe. Sally, after what seemed aeons of time, managed to reach Luke, and kneel down beside him, and touch him. All in slow motion, every movement taking hours and hours ... He was breathing, face deathly white, blood seeping into the red gravel around him. And, as Wilma's face appeared, Sally fell to the ground in a dead faint.

She opened her eyes to find herself on a settee in the drawing room. Wilma bent over her, holding a face flannel. 'You all right, honey?'

'Yes.' Sally struggled to sit up. 'Luke—where's Luke——?' Her voice rose in hysteria and she clutched Wilma's arm.

'Shush, the doctor's with him now, upstairs.'

'I must go.' She managed to stand, leaning on Wilma. 'He—saved my life—he saved——'

'Don't talk, honey. We got a good idea what happened. She drove up after you—she tried to kill you——'

'I know. I didn't realise, I thought it was someone coming to see Luke. Then he was running towards me, and he shouted something, I remember that—and—and he pushed me, and the c-car hit him instead——'

'She's dead, honey.'

The shock was too great; Sally nearly fell, only Wilma's strong arm saving her. 'She'll bother you no more, Lord rest her soul. She drove on, and over the cliff—they just found her car——'

'I think I'm going to be sick——' whispered Sally.

'Come on with me, then, and after we'll go up to Mr Vilis.'

'Is he—was he hurt badly?'

'We don't know yet. But he's strong and he's tough, and he opened his eyes and looked at me when we got him upstairs, and he said: "Is she all right? I tried to push her to safety——" so you see, honey, he's well enough to worry about you—and as soon as you see him, why, that'll make him a whole heap better.'

Wilma took Sally into a cloakroom with a basin on the ground floor, where she bathed her face.

'It's all right—it's passed now. Take me up, Wilma.'

Slowly they climbed the stairs, and into the bedroom. A doctor and a nurse bent over Luke, and John just stood inside the door, his face a mask of shock.

The doctor turned. 'Mrs Vilis? Will you come and reassure your husband that you're safe? Then perhaps we can persuade him to let us give him a tranquilliser.'

Sally walked over to see Luke, his face ghastly white, head and one side of his face bandaged, lying against the pillows.

'I'm here, Luke,' she said softly. 'You saved my life.'

'Good.' His mouth barely moved, and she saw the agony in his eyes. 'I—can—sleep—now. Don't leave —me.'

'I won't. I'll stay here, I promise.'

She nodded to the doctor, who stuck a needle in Luke's arm. Seconds later, he was asleep. Sally stayed, calm amidst the bustle that surrounded her; talk of portable X-ray machines, and blood replacement and treatment for shock washed around and over her but didn't touch her. For he was going to be all right. He would live. And she was going to stay with him until he was better. She sat quietly at the side of the bed and watched all the activity, more people arriving, two more nurses, X-ray machine, another doctor, apparatus for giving blood, and she held Luke's hand, and only when Wilma at last took hold of her and said: 'You're coming down for some food. It won't take but a few minutes,' did she at last allow herself to be led away.

That night she slept in a small bed in the same room as Luke, while a nurse guarded him at the other side, and a doctor slept in the room next to them.

In the cool watches of the night Sally awoke, and heard his quiet, steady breathing, and she thought, I love him, and he saved my life and nearly got killed himself, and I can't leave him now, not until he's better. And on that thought she fell asleep again.

She thought about it when she had a bath the following morning. Talitha was dead, and she had been one of the main reasons for Luke's marriage. Sally had learned a kind of humility—and that had been another reason. And the third and last reason was that she reminded him in some way of the only woman he had ever loved. But that was too unbearable. And until he was better, and walking about, Sally would stay— on that she was decided. He would find no fault with her, because there would be none. She would read to him, talk to him, wash him and care for him, because she owed him her life. She loved him, but she would never tell him that, for it had not been in their agreement, and he might find it too amusing for words, and that would be even more unbearable. And so, calmly, Sally thought out her plans: they would work out, because they had to.

She went straight back into the bedroom after her bath. Wilma would bring up her breakfast there and while she ate it, the nurse would go down for hers. In this way, Luke would never be left alone, even for a minute. He had been X-rayed, and given blood, and he lay there in a kind of half sleep, and watched her cross the room towards him.

'How are you this morning?' Sally asked quietly.

It was clearly an effort for him to listen. She held her breath, wondering if she should not have spoken, but when she looked in silent appeal at the plump middle-aged nurse, she was met with a nod and a smile.

'Don't talk too much, Mrs Vilis,' the other said quietly. 'He's under sedation, but it's good for him to know that you're here. If it's all right with you, I'll go down for my breakfast now.'

'Yes, of course.' Sally bent over Luke. 'Don't answer if it's difficult,' she said gently. 'I'll just sit quietly here for a while.'

He murmured something that was inaudible and she leaned nearer. Faintly the words came: 'I didn't mean this to happen.'

'Of course you didn't!' She smiled. 'I know that. I just—wish I'd been quicker at realising who it was in the car, and none of this would have happened. I would have got out of the way, and you—would have been—safe.' She closed her eyes. Dear God, she thought. He could have died, and it would have been while saving me.

She sat down beside the bed, and he tried to move his head, and his breathing became quicker. Sally sensed his distress, and instinctively she reached out her hand and touched his. 'I'm here,' she said. 'I'm sitting beside you. Try and rest.' His fingers moved, closed over her hand, and then he was still. It was as though he gave a sigh of contentment.

Then, suddenly, Sally thought she knew why, and the sensation was like icy water trickling down her spine. He was drugged, semi-conscious—and he thought she was Laura. His breathing became more steady, his eyes closed, but still he held her hand as he slipped into sleep, and it was like that when the doctor came in several minutes later. Sally's arm was uncomfortable and going dead, but not for anything would she have moved it.

The doctor spoke quietly: 'The housekeeper is bringing you some food up, Mrs Vilis. He's asleep—you needn't remain there.'

She very gently moved her hand, a fraction of an inch at a time, and the sleeping man didn't stir, only sighed softly once, and she wondered what dreams he was having of Laura, and she thought: if this is to be a continuation of my punishment, it will be more difficult than anything that has gone before—but I shan't falter in any way. I'll manage. I can cope with anything now, after all that's happened. I'll survive.

'Thank you, doctor,' she said. 'Have the X-ray re-sults come in yet?'

'Yes. One of his legs is broken, and two ribs, and he has severe concussion, but he's a very strong man and he will be well looked after. In a few weeks your hus-band will be back to normal, Mrs Vilis, I can assure you.'

Wilma gave a perfunctory tap and came in with a tray. 'Now you eat all this up, Mrs Vilis,' she said, and smiled at Sally.

'I'll try—but I don't promise.'

'Then I'll wait and watch, and see you do. You've got to keep your strength up.' A look was exchanged be-tween housekeeper and doctor, who nodded his agree-ment.

'Indeed yes. What would your husband think if we allowed you to get run down? We'd all get our march-ing orders, and speedily too, and that would never do. He needs you here by his side, and that can get very tiring after a while. So you must do as Wilma says.' He went over to his black bag and opened it. 'I suggest you take two of these with your food, once a day,' and he handed her a bottle of tablets.

'What are they?' Sally asked.

'Vitamins and iron. Two with your breakfast every day, remember now.' He looked at his watch. 'I'll go and phone my colleague downstairs, if I may.'

'Of course.' Sally began to pick at the crispy rolls. What had he said? 'He needs you here by his side.' If only he knew the truth of it! But there was only one who did, Rosa, and she wasn't here. Sally wondered if anyone had told them what had happened, and asked the waiting Wilma, after the doctor had gone out.

'Yes, ma'am,' said Wilma. 'John drove over last night to tell them the news. I thought it better he should go rather than telephone. Mrs Herrick answered the door and said she'd tell your uncle. She was very upset and said you were to call her as soon you felt able to, and if you wanted her, she'd be right over.'

'Thanks. I'll phone her later. I'd like to see them.' Sally's lip trembled, and she put down the roll she had been trying vainly to eat.

'Why, honey, what is it?' Wilma was beside her instantly, moving the tray away, her face filled with concern. 'He's going to be all right——'

'I know. It's not that——' she fought to control the threatening tears, suddenly overwhelmed in the strangest way, and by nothing she could put into words. 'It's—it's——' She caught Wilma's hand.

'There, there, why don't you lie down for a while, and then eat? I'll watch Mr Vilis till the nurse comes back. You're suffering from shock—and no wonder, after all that's happened. A rest will do you good.'

'It won't—nothing will. You—you don't understand——'

'Sure I do. Why, a lot of women in your place would have just taken to their beds, and needed treatment.'

Perhaps, thought Sally numbly, she was right. Maybe I am suffering from shock. Someone tries to kill me —that's enough, just knowing there's all that hate stored up in another person—but it was more as well, so much more. And she couldn't tell Wilma, or Rosa, or anyone. For how could you say, I've fallen in love

with a man who has contempt for me? 'I don't need
to lie down, thanks, Wilma,' she managed at last. 'I'll
stay here.' She took a deep shuddering breath. 'And
I'll eat my breakfast, like a good girl.' She even managed to smile. But she wasn't able to see Wilma's face
as the housekeeper left the room, or to guess at the
thoughts in the other woman's mind.

There was a routine established; smoothly and imperceptibly it had been worked out, and as the days
passed, things became easier. For Sally's own deter-
mination and will power gradually overcame her de-
pression of the morning, and Wilma remarked on the
change in her after lunch as she removed the plates
from the dining room table.

'Mrs Vilis, you're looking so much better now, I'm
delighted. I sure was concerned about you this morning.' She shook her head. 'So I asked the doctor to keep
an eye on you.'

Sally smiled. 'I wondered why he kept frowning at
me! He and the nurse have been very good. They
ordered me out of the bedroom and told me to take a
walk round the garden while they washed and shaved
Luke—though how they managed with that bandage
on his face I can't imagine. And they won't let me sit
with him for longer than an hour at a time at present.'
She gave a wry smile. 'No one's ever ordered me about
before, but I'd hate to answer that nurse back. She
looks as though she's used to being obeyed.'

'She's the Sister in Charge at the hospital on the
next island,' answered Wilma. 'And believe me, she
can be a tartar—but she's the best nurse in the world.

She'll look after Mr Vilis like he was her own son. You'll see the difference in a few days.'

'I can see it already. He was so ill last night—now he's swearing at her because she won't let him sit up. They had a right old row just before I came down.' Sally smiled reflectively. 'Luke lost! He's still lying there managing to look very obstinate—but doing precisely what she tells him.

Wilma chuckled. 'He'll be walking around in a few days—broken leg or no, you'll see. Then the sparks will fly. The doctor will keep out of the way, if he knows what's good for him, mark my words.'

'But it's impossible—how——'

'Honey, *nothing's* impossible where he's concerned. That man is made of steel.'

Sally looked into the other woman's eyes, and a spark of understanding and warmth was exchanged. 'I think I know that already,' she said slowly.

'Sure you do. He's your husband, isn't he? But I'll bet he never told you about the time he was in a plane crash—about five years ago?'

'No.' Her heart thudded painfully. 'What—happened?'

'He wasn't the pilot, only a passenger. The plane came down in some hills, caught in a freak storm. He was flung clear of the wreckage, and even though he was injured, he went back into the plane to pull out the pilot and a woman and child who were trapped inside. Got himself messed up terrible, but he saved their lives, 'cos two minutes later the plane went up in flames.'

'Oh, my God! Yet he still flies?'

'He made himself go up immediately after—said it was the only way. Soon as they let him out of the hospital bed he was off on a plane—so you see, he and Sister Andrews are like old friends. She knows how stubborn he is—and he knows just how much he can get away with.'

'You mean—she's looked after him before?' Sally asked.

'Yes. Said she'd never had such a bad patient—but as soon as the doc contacted her, she came over here like a shot.'

Sally laughed. 'A bad patient? I can see what she means. It must be a challenge to her to have someone like Luke to look after.' She felt as if a burden had been lifted from her. She couldn't have explained why, but the feeling was there. And for the present, it was enough. He would be all right, she knew that deep down inside her now. He saved my life, she thought, and I wasn't the first—and both times he had been hurt—and he's stronger than anyone I've ever known, and because of that he'll survive. He'll always survive. And when I go, it won't matter at all. That thought was a sobering one, and she put her hand on the table, because it was time for her to go back to the bedroom and sit with Luke while Sister Andrews had a break.

'You all right, honey?' The other woman's voice was soft with concern.

She nodded. 'Yes, I'm fine. I'm going back now. Do you think he'd like me to read to him?'

Wilma's face creased in a grin. 'Bet he would. You've seen the library here? All Mr Vilis's books—and all well read.'

'Then I'll go and ask him. Thanks for the lunch,

Wilma. I'll phone my aunt and uncle in a little while and ask them over.' Sally left the room and walked slowly up the stairs and into the bedroom—slap into the middle of a slight argument.

Sister Andrews's voice was low, but it carried authority. 'No, Mr Vilis, you may not!' She turned at Sally's entrance. 'Mrs Vilis, will you tell your husband that he's too poorly to make telephone calls at present?'

Sally walked over to the bed. 'I'll make any calls for you,' she said quietly, 'if you'll tell me who you want phoning.'

Luke looked at her. For a moment of time, it was as if they were alone. All that had been, everything that had happened, was caught in that look, and Sally saw the strength returning, saw in his eyes the toughness inherent in him, and marvelled at his powers of recovery.

'You can't,' he said flatly. 'How do you know what I want to say?'

'I don't until you tell me,' she answered calmly, and added, turning to the waiting nurse: 'Wilma has your lunch ready, Sister. I'll stay with my husband now and sort out his nonsense about phone calls.' She gave the woman a little smile, which was returned.

'Fine. I'll leave you to him.' Sister Andrews rolled her eyes heavenwards. 'He's feeling better—he's started arguing with me. That's always a good sign.' She stared at Luke. 'I've never had a patient like you.'

He returned the stare. 'That makes two of us. I've never had a nurse like you.'

The snort that was heard muffled through the door, as the Sister left the room, could have been one of annoyance—or laughter. 'Just tell me,' said Sally, 'and

I'll telephone anyone you like, and say what you want me to say. *Then* I'll read to you—if you want me to.'

There was silence for a moment. Then: 'Right. Get a notepad and pen—and listen.'

Sally fetched a writing pad and pen from the table by the window, and stood by the bed. 'Ready when you are,' she said cheerfully. 'Fire away.'

'God, you're as bossy as that bloody nurse,' Luke grumbled.

'Really? I must remember not to be. Are you ready yet, or do you want to give me a lecture first?' she smiled.

Something that might have been a grin touched the corners of his mouth. 'Okay. First number——' and he began to reel off names and numbers at a rate that had Sally writing at full strength to keep up with him. When he had finished the list, he added: 'You're to tell them I want them here tomorrow at two.'

'Oh, but,' she protested, 'I don't think—we'll have to ask the doctor or Sister Andrews——'

'Damn them!' he grated. 'If I say they're to come here, they come. I'm not a child, you know. This is my house, and I'm the master of it——'

'And at the moment you're a patient, and you're injured, and being looked after, and if they say you can't have visitors then——' She stopped as he caught her arm.

'Listen, Sally, if they say I can't see anyone, then *you* can do all the talking. Dammit, I've a business to run—several, in fact—and I don't intend to lie here twiddling my thumbs for the next few days—do I make myself clear?'

'Haven't you always? All right, I'll see them if you can't. And I'll say exactly what you tell me to. Will that satisfy you?'

'Yes.' Clearly the effort of speaking had tired him. His face was white, and the fire had gone from his eyes. Sally felt a rush of love for him, mingling with sympathy, and very gently she took his hand.

'It's all right,' she said very softly. 'I'll help you in any way I can. After all, it's because of me you're there.' Her eyes filled with tears which she made no effort to hide. 'I'm sorry, Luke, I won't shout at you again. I'll go and phone when Sister Andrews returns.'

He looked up at her, and then at her hand on his. And suddenly his face changed. Anxiously she whispered: 'Are you in pain?'

'No.' The word came out as a whisper. 'Not pain. It's—nothing.'

She sighed. For a precious moment, she had sensed a tenderness about him, and then it was gone. 'Just lie there and rest. What would you like me to read to you later?'

'Do I have a choice?' He grinned faintly.

'Of course! I'm yours to command,' she said blithely.

'You'll find it in the library—Wilma will show you. Short stories by Neil Munro—*Para-Handy Tales*. They're my weakness.'

'How strange! And mine too. I'll enjoy reading them. Rest now, I'll sit quietly here, then I'll make your calls for you.' He took her hand and squeezed it gently. 'Thank you.' It was enough. It was more than enough.

# CHAPTER NINE

NOTHING could have prepared Sally for what was to happen the following day at two in the afternoon. She had telephoned all the people Luke had asked her to, and the calls had gone out to places all over the world, some she had never heard of, others to London, Toronto, Sydney, even one to Rio de Janeiro. And to every one she had said what Luke had told her to say, and every one had agreed that he would be there—a total of fifteen men in all.

She had called Rosa and Uncle Alistair, and they made a visit later that evening. To Sally there was a definite change in Rosa; a hitherto unsuspected warmth, a caring. They had not stayed long, but they had drunk wine, and eaten some of Wilma's delicious small cakes, and had paid a brief call to Luke. Sally felt much better after their departure, and a warmth inside her. It was in a strange way as if she had found a friend in Rosa. It was a comfortable feeling.

She had also read for a while to Luke—but had been forced to stop when laughter threatened to undo all the good his nurse had done. Sally had put the book down, stifling her own laughter at a particularly outrageous and colourful incident in one of the book's short tales. 'It's no good,' she had said. 'I'll have Sister

Andrews after me if you have a relapse.'

'Damn her,' he had muttered. 'Carry on reading.'

'No. Later.' Sally was surprised at her own firmness. 'When you've recovered. Anyway, you've got to tell me what to say to this crowd that's coming to-morrow——'

'Hell! Oh, all right. Get a notebook.' Then he told her.

She waited by the window. Two o'clock, he had said, and it was a quarter to the hour now. Sister Andrews had given him a sound scolding when the news of the impending arrivals had leaked out via Wilma, who had asked him, in all innocence, if the fifteen were to be accommodated at the house, and had been over-heard by not only the nurse but the doctor as well. Sally had left the room hastily in the ensuing battle, returning to find all calm and serene. The ripples had closed over the incident. Luke had won. But it was Sally who was going to be doing all the work. It was a challenge, and she was filled, as she stood at the bed-room window looking out, with a kind of inner strength, a purpose. She was going to have to cope with fifteen hard-headed businessmen, all a part of Luke's empire, who probably wouldn't take kindly to being given instructions by a woman. Sally had no illusions about that. She smiled to herself, and Luke must have been watching, for he said: 'What are you laughing about?'

She turned, cool, self-possessed. 'I'm not laughing, I'm smiling. I'm wondering how they'll react to me giving them instructions.'

'Are you worried?'

She shook her head. 'No.'

'Come over here.' Sally obediently crossed to the bed.

'Yes? What do you want? They'll be arriving at any time.' She looked down at him lying white-faced in the bed, and the love she had hidden inside her welled up so that for a moment she was frightened it might show in her eyes.

'Just to tell you—thanks.'

'I haven't done anything yet.'

'But you will,' he assured her. 'You'll manage everything admirably.'

She nodded, 'I know,' and saw the grin on his face.

'You're like me in a lot of ways,' he said, as if in surprise.

'I'm not. I'm not like you at all.' The fragile mood that had, for a few moments, seemed to fill the room, a mood of warmth and love, was shattered. Sally moved slightly away. She didn't want him to say any more, and was startled at her own reaction. Luke, as if he too sensed something, looked hard at her, and his eyes went as cold and dangerous as they could be at certain times.

'Perhaps you're not,' he agreed. 'That was a stupid thing to say. You must blame the drugs I'm on.'

She took a deep breath. 'Yes. Now you'd better rest for a while. I'm going down to welcome the first arrivals when they come. Wilma has converted the dining room into something approaching a boardroom —you'd be proud of her. The table is set out with papers, the tape recorder is ready to record everything that's said, and John has filled the container of iced water you asked for.' Her voice was briskly efficient, even to her own ears, and that was just the way she intended to keep it. 'So unless you've any last-minute instructions I'll leave you, and call Sister Andrews in.'

'Just one thing,' he said. 'Good luck.'

She smiled. 'Do you think I'll need it? They don't frighten me. *I'm* Mrs Vilis, remember? Your wife.' And she smiled softly as she turned away.

The first three men arrived, and shortly after them, another four, and the drive was filled with the sound of cars hastily reversing to go back to the airstrip for further arrivals. Sally, as she conducted the tough-looking, well-dressed men into the dining room, marvelled at the efficiency of Luke's organisation, and the speed with which everything he planned happened.

She smiled at the seven waiting men watching her, cool-eyed, hard. 'Do sit down, gentlemen,' she said quietly. 'The housekeeper will be in with drinks in a moment——' she waved her arm, 'and there's iced water over there. I won't go into any details until the rest have arrived, but on behalf of my husband I'd like to welcome you to Vilis House.'

'You're Mrs Vilis?' asked one of them.

'Yes.'

'Hank Martin, New York office. Pleased to meet you.' Tall, lanky, crew-cut, he was more friendly—or appeared to be—than the other men. They shook hands, and then the others, taking their cue, did the same, introducing themselves as they did so. Wilma wheeled in the loaded trolley of drinks and the next few minutes were spent observing the social niceties.

Small talk was exchanged. Several of the men knew one another, and as more arrived. Sally began to remember names and form impressions.

When at last they were all seated there, she took her seat at the head of the table as if it were something she had been doing every day of her life, switched on the tape recorder, and began to speak the words that Luke had told her to.

'Gentlemen,' she said, 'I'm here today on behalf of my husband Luke Vilis, who, as I told you all briefly on the telephone, was involved a couple of days ago in an accident. He was not badly hurt, and will shortly be up and about——' She paused, looking round the room. Every man's attention was upon her. All sat still, no movement, no fidgeting, and listened to her intently. She took a deep breath, fighting a brief moment of sheer dizzying panic. What on *earth* was she doing sitting there spouting? But the moment passed, and she smiled. 'But during those first hours after his accident, he had time to think, and to realise that he could, for one reason or another, be put out of action for a while, and that the smooth running of his many business interests must not be allowed to be disrupted. That's why he has asked you to be here.' She paused deliberately. The proverbial pin could have dropped, and it would have sounded like an explosion, so silent was the room. She wondered if they had all stopped breathing. 'Because he has decided to appoint a second-in-command, someone who can—and is willing—to take over the reins if at any time he's unable to do so.'

The room erupted as everyone began to talk at once.

Sally sat there calmly. Luke had warned her. He had known what would happen and had told her to sit quietly, and to listen, and this she did. There was one man he had told her to keep an eye on, to observe, and to remember and tell him. She watched this man now—Craig Lamont, from Luke's organisation in the South of France, a tall grey-haired, powerfully built man, he was the only one not actively engaged in the hubbub around him. He sat there, silent, impassive, and watched. Then for a moment he looked across at Sally, and the cool green eyes met hers, and he grinned very briefly. And she knew why Luke had asked her to watch him. She knew who he had in mind—and she knew that this was the right man. She stood up.

'Will you excuse me, gentlemen?' Her voice cut across the noise, and it was stilled. 'Mr Lamont, my husband would like a word with you. Will you come with me?'

He rose to his feet. 'Yes, ma'am, I will.' He was a Canadian, and he followed her out of the room, closing out the new uproar as he shut the door, and looked at Sally. 'You did very well,' he told her.

She stumbled, and would have fallen had he not caught her arm. 'You okay, ma'am?' he asked anxiously.

'I'm fine, thanks. That noise—Luke warned me—but——'

'You dropped a bombshell, that's all. They'll get over it. Now, which way, Mrs Vilis?'

She took him up into the bedroom where Luke waited, and across to the bed. 'He's here, Luke,' she said. 'You were right.'

The two men shook hands, Sister Andrews stood up and smoothed her apron and looked accusingly at Craig Lamont. 'He's sick,' she said. 'Don't you get him upset now.'

Craig smiled at her and laid his hand on his heart. 'Ma'am, I swear I won't,' he said, and Sister Andrews visibly wilted under the force of that smile.

'Why don't you and Sally go and get a drink?' Luke said quietly. 'Leave that crowd to fight it out. Your job's done, Sally, for now. Craig will take over when he goes down—right, Craig?'

'Right, Luke,' Craig grinned.

Without saying a word—it was doubtful if either could have done so—Sally and Sister Andrews left the room. Luke's parting words followed them. 'I'll ring when I want you back.' Sally went down the stairs with the nurse, and as if at some unspoken signal they both made their way towards the welcome of Wilma's kitchen.

Afterwards, it was all subtly different. The bell rang several minutes later when all three women sat at the table sipping iced tea with lemon.

Sally swallowed hers hurriedly. 'That's for me.'

Sister Andrews rose. 'I'll come too. Thank you, Wilma.'

'You're welcome.' Wilma's face creased in a grin. 'Lordy, you hear that noise? Shall I take them all some more drinks?'

'Before I get down again? Hmm, yes. I think, somehow, they're all going to need one. Thanks, Wilma.'

They went upstairs, and Craig turned as they entered the room.

'Okay, Sally, you can take him down again,' said Luke. 'Just introduce him—and then stand clear. Craig will take over the meeting. You can stay and listen, or not, as you choose. Whatever you decide, put in a new cassette tape first, I want it all on record.'

'Yes, Luke. Are you ready, Mr Lamont?'

'Ready, ma'am.' He turned to Luke. 'I won't let you down—ever.'

'I know you won't. I knew before—but I needed everyone together to tell them all so. You'll be up afterwards to tell me everything?'

'I will. Mrs Vilis? After you, ma'am.' Craig held open the door, and Sally went out.

As Craig opened the dining room door a sudden hush fell. Sally walked in, head held high. 'Gentlemen,' she said, 'my husband and Mr Lamont have had a talk, and he has something to tell you. Mr Lamont, will you sit in my place?'

He nodded. 'Thank you, Mrs Vilis.' Sally, aware that every eye was now on the tall Canadian, put in a new tape on the cassette, and took the old one from it.

'I'll leave you now,' she said. 'Thank you. Wilma has given you more drinks. Please help yourselves whenever you wish.'

She walked to the door, and Craig Lamont held it for her. She nodded her thanks, and stood for a moment outside when it was closed again. She heard him begin: 'Gentlemen, Mr Vilis has appointed me as his second-in-command. I'm sure we'll all want to discuss it—and to do so with the minimum of fuss. I'll go round the table. Everyone will have a chance to express their opinion individually. Right, Bob, you first——'

The voice faded as Sally moved away. She discovered to her dismay that she was shaking, and didn't understand why. Clutching the cassette, she ran upstairs to tell Luke all that had happened.

He listened as she went through the events since the first arrivals, and when she had finished he asked her for her impressions of the various men, which she gave him. It was beginning to seem unreal, faintly like a dream in which she had no part, but was merely an observer. Even Luke seemed unreal, and his voice grew fainter, and the room seemed to be filled with shadows——

'Sally!' his voice brought her sharply back. 'What's wrong? You're as white as a sheet.'

'I——' she couldn't speak. The room was going round; everything was covered in grey mist. Her last recollection, before she fainted, was hearing Sister Andrews's voice come from a great distance:

'All right, child, just relax——'

Then she was lying on a cool bed, and the nurse bent over her, holding her pulse. She smiled at Sally. 'You've done enough today, Mrs Vilis. It's bed for you.'

'But where am I?'

'In the room next to your husband's. And here you'll stay.'

'But——' Sally began.

'No buts. I'm in charge here, and you're not fit to

be sitting reading, and taking meetings. Whatever next?'

Sally gave her a weak smile. 'I'll be fine in a——'

'You'll be fine tomorrow, yes. But until then you'll stay here and do as I tell you. Now swallow these.' 'These' were two white pills held in the nurse's hand, and a glass of water was waiting by the bed. Sally, recognising defeat when she saw it, took them and swallowed them. 'Now you'll sleep, and when you wake in the morning you'll be as right as rain. I'll keep looking in—Mr Vilis won't let me in peace if I don't.'

The room was drifting, as in a mist, and Sally began to feel very pleasant and cool, but it was too much effort to think anyway, and that nice Canadian would probably take care of everything. Luke would soon be better, and wasn't it odd that he should be concerned anyway ... Sally slept. And slept, and slept.

She awoke to the cool grey light of pre-dawn to hear the silence of the house washing around her. Someone had covered her with a sheet, and she pushed it aside and sat up. She felt much better and incredibly hungry.

Padding downstairs, barefooted so as not to waken anyone, she went into the kitchen and buttered a piece of bread, poured out a glass of milk, and sat down to eat. Soon she must see Rosa. Soon she would have to leave—perhaps it might be before Luke was up and about, for if Craig Lamont stayed, and was in a position to relieve Luke of the inevitable pressure of business, she would be under no obligation. And she must leave. If she was to retain any shreds of self-respect and dignity, it must be before it was too late. For it was

Laura, always had been, always would be, of whom he thought; whom he loved.

I can't be second best, thought Sally. And I can't fight a ghost. Even Talitha would have been preferable. But now she too was gone.

She sat and looked out of the window, and rubbed the back of her neck, which ached. I'll phone them today, she thought, and see when they're going—and see how soon I too can leave here. After a while life would resume its normal pattern, and all would be the same as before. Only, even as she had the thought, she knew it wouldn't. She herself had changed, she knew that deep within her. It was not the marriage itself; not just that. It was far more, and now, as she gazed out of the room, she seemed to see the shallowness of her life, the empty seeking of pleasure, and knew it had come to an end.

Whatever happened to her in the future, she would not go back to that, to the endless round of parties, country weekends, night-clubbing into the small hours, the inevitable sleeping it off, then shopping for more clothes, because it didn't do to wear the same thing too often . . .

'So there you are! You shouldn't give me a fright like that!' The accusing voice came from the doorway, and Sister Andrews marched across the room, saw the half eaten sandwich, the half empty glass of milk, and snorted. 'Why didn't you call me? Mr Vilis was going frantic when he heard me call you——'

'I didn't want to wake anyone,' Sally protested feebly.

'Well, you did! And you'd better go in and see your

husband before he fires me. He's had a terrible night, very feverish. I warned him——'

'Is he all right?' she turned wide eyes on the nurse.

'He's fine—or will be when he sees you. Come along, Mrs Vilis, I'll get Wilma to bring you up a nice breakfast soon. She'll be about any time now.'

Luke worried. Luke *concerned*? Perhaps, after a feverish night, he had her confused with someone else. And she knew who. She stood up.

'Yes, Sister, I'm coming up now. I feel fine.'

'So you should, my dear. Those two pills knocked you out for long enough to rest you completely. I might even allow you to read to Mr Vilis later.'

She wasn't joking. She was perfectly serious. Feeling like a schoolgirl who has just received a scolding, followed by a pat on the head from the teacher, Sally meekly allowed herself to be taken upstairs.

Luke was waiting for her. He struggled to sit up when she went in alone. 'Where the hell have you been?' he demanded.

She stared back at him. 'Downstairs for a glass of milk. Why?'

'You were supposed to stay in bed.'

'And I didn't, did I? Perhaps I am like you after all, disobeying nurse's instructions.' She glared hard at him. He pushed the bedclothes to one side and heaved himself up even further.

'Damn this bed! I'm getting up today——'

'You can't——' she began.

'Watch me!' he grated. 'Just watch me.'

'How will you walk? You've got one leg in plaster——'

'Ever heard of wheelchairs?' Sally saw the whiteness of his face, even against the bandages, saw the strain, even as she saw the strength of him, and she went over and knelt beside the bed.

'You mustn't try. You're not ready——'

'Then it should be interesting.'

'I'll read to you——' she began.

'And then what? Lying here, wondering what's going on? That's not for me, Sally. I don't wait for anything. I'm getting up later, whether the doc or the nurse says I may or not.' He caught her hand. 'It's quite simple. I tell myself I can do it, therefore I can.'

She felt his strength in the grip, and responded with her own. He always did what he said he would.

'All right, I'll help you,' she sighed.

'Will you? How?'

'Anything you like. I'll push the wheelchair, I'll help you get in and out of it, I'll sit in with the men with you so I can——'

'Why?' The blunt question took her by surprise. And if she answered, 'Because I love you,' he would probably have fallen out of bed laughing.

'Because you're so determined. Why else?'

The answer didn't satisfy him, she could see that, and she saw the hard shrewd eyes assessing her swiftly, and felt as if he might be able to read her mind, and was uneasy. To cover up, to say anything to change the subject, she added: 'How will we get the chair downstairs?—I'm strong, but I'm not that strong.'

'There's a lift, didn't you know? I thought you'd seen all round the house, for God's sake.'

'Er—oh!' Then she remembered. 'So there is! I'd

forgotten. Okay, where's the chair?'

'John will go for it after breakfast. When I make up my mind I don't waste time.'

'I know.' She said it very quietly, and for a few moments afterwards there was silence. It filled the room, it spilled round them—and the words seemed to softly echo in the air: I know, I know. Luke opened his mouth to say something—and the doctor walked in. Sally would never know what he had been going to say.

The doctor wore nightclothes, and had clearly been woken up by Sister Andrews, and he was looking faintly annoyed—an expression that changed to alarm when he saw Luke sitting half out of bed.

'Mr Vilis!' he exclaimed. 'What are you doing?'

'Getting into practice, doctor—for when I get up later on today.'

'I forbid it—I absolutely——'

'Yes.' Luke's voice effectively cut in. 'You wouldn't be much of a doctor if you didn't. Point taken, doc. But you don't know me.'

Doctor Rossi looked in silent appeal at Sally. 'Oh, but I do, Mr Vilis,' he answered. 'Only too well. I've sent Sister Andrews off for the day, and I'm going to telephone for another nurse in a few minutes. You need three or four to control you, I think. I am responsible for you, remember, and I say you're not strong enough to even think of getting out of bed for several days.'

'Want to bet?' jeered Luke.

The doctor pursed his lips. 'I don't gamble.'

'But this is one you can't lose, doc. I get up, I'm fine

—you owe me, say, a bottle of wine. I get up, I'm *not* okay, so you've won—you'll get a thousand dollars extra to your fee—*and* complete obedience until you say I'm better.' He grinned at the doctor. 'Well?'

A silent battle was on. Then: 'You are the most obstinate, stubborn patient I have ever known. And I shall put that on my report.'

'You do that, doctor. Is the bet on or not?'

'You give me no choice. I can't forcibly detain you in bed—except by drugging you, and the sooner you can do without, the better. But I warn you, I shall be watching you keenly, every minute, and if you show any strain, it's back to bed.'

'Agreed.'

Doctor Rossi nodded. 'Now, let me take your pulse and blood pressure. Mrs Vilis, if you'll excuse us?'

'Of course. I'll go and have a shower.' Sally fled.

Under the cool sparkling water, as she soaped herself, she saw again Luke's face when he had spoken to the doctor, and a small excitement grew inside her. Luke was clever. He wouldn't attempt too much; but he would have his way, of that she was convinced. And she would help him. She wondered again what he had been about to say when the doctor interrupted. The atmosphere had been taut, had built up to a fine pitch of awareness—and the words would have been significant, she sensed that much. But they had gone for ever. She stepped out of the shower and began to pat herself dry on the fluffy white towel.

The sun was high in the sky, but they sat in the shelter of a large tree, and it was cooler. Luke sat in the chair, Sally beside him on a bench, and Craig Lamont next to her. A bee hummed nearby, searching among the flowers for nectar, and far in the distance a plane droned across the white sky. It was mid-afternoon, and the atmosphere was tranquil and calm.

'Smoke, Luke?' Craig offered him a cheroot. 'With your permission, Mrs Vilis?'

'Of course,' she smiled. 'Shall I leave you two to talk? I'll go and entertain the others, shall I?'

'They'll manage. They're in the pool, aren't they, Craig?' was Luke's answer.

'Some of them. The rest are sprawled out sipping Bacardis and Cokes and muttering dark things about me.' Craig laughed. 'I can take it. Everything's gone off very well, as a matter of fact. I think they're all adjusted to the idea of a number two boss . . .'

Sally sat there, only half listening as the two men talked, letting it wash over her without actually touching her. He had done it—Luke had done it. But she had known he would. She glanced casually at him. The bandages were gone from his head, only a small plaster remained, the hair shaved away around it. That would soon grow. There was a scar on his left cheek, but that, Doctor Rossi had told her, would fade in time. He wore sunglasses, which lent him a slightly sinister aspect, and he had protested, but Doctor Rossi had been insistent.

The new nurse had arrived, a younger, stricter version of Sister Andrews—if that were possible—and had been horrified by what Luke intended to do. But somehow, after talking to him for a few minutes, her protests had died away. He can charm when he wants to, thought Sally, and smiled to herself. Oh yes, he has charm. I've seen it in action. She tried to remember that first impression of him—big, lean, dangerous. He was still all three, despite the accident. Dangerous— and now she knew fully why. Dangerous to me, she thought, to my heart, to my very being. For he has changed me, and made me love him in a way I never thought possible, but at least he'll never know, never know——

She blinked, opened her eyes, and looked at Luke. 'What did you say?' she asked.

'Weren't you listening?'

'No.' She could say that with truth. 'When you started talking business, I drifted off into my own thoughts.'

'I asked if you'd go and get us a drink. Anything will do. I don't think I'm allowed alcohol, so something long and cool for me. Craig, what about you?'

'The same, Luke. I like a clear head during the day,' Craig laughed.

Sally stood up. 'Of course. I'll go now. Excuse me.' She walked away, and before she was out of earshot, heard Craig's words to Luke.

'Your wife is one of the most attractive women I've ever seen.' She had to go on walking. To have hesitated then would have been most obvious. But she would have loved to have heard Luke's reply—if, of course, he bothered to answer at all.

She went into the kitchen. Wilma had two island girls helping her with the extra guests, and all were busy preparing dinner for that evening. Wilma looked up from dissecting a chicken. 'Why, Mrs Vilis,' she said, 'I was just coming out for you with the message. Your aunt, Mrs Herrick, telephoned just a few minutes ago. She'd like you to call her as soon as you can.'

'I'll do it now. And I'd like a large jug of something cold to drink—no alcohol, and three glasses. I won't be a moment.' She went out hurriedly, picked up the telephone in the privacy of Luke's study, and dialled Rosa's number. She had the feeling that she knew what she was to hear.

'Sally? That was quick. I thought I'd let you know the news at once. I didn't say anything to the house-keeper, of course. It's all fixed up. We go in ten days. Alistair is seeing a specialist in London—and, oh, Sally, this man is marvellous! There's a chance for Alistair. Isn't that wonderful?'

'I'm so glad. Thanks for telling me, Rosa. Before you go—and we'll meet before then, of course—don't forget to slip me your address in London. But quietly, of course.'

'I know. I have to make a few more phone calls—but you wanted to know first. Can you call round to-morrow—any time?'

'I'll try,' said Sally. 'I must go now. Luke's waiting for a drink. 'Bye, Rosa.'

' 'Bye, Sally.'

Sally put the telephone down. Ten days. In ten days she would be free. Free.

# CHAPTER TEN

THEY were alone in the bedroom. It was evening, and the swift darkness had fallen, and Luke was back in bed after a triumphant debut. He was obviously, and not surprisingly, tired. He lay back on the pillow and looked up at Sally sitting beside the bed, book on knee.

'Come and lie down beside me,' he invited. She looked at him.

'But I'm reading to you.'

'Damn the book. I'm too sleepy to listen. Do as I tell you.' Despite his tiredness, a touch of the old arrogance was back. She shrugged. What did it matter? Ten days would pass very quickly. She slipped off her sandals and lay on top of the bed beside him. Then she saw his eyes upon her, and he reached out a hand and traced a finger down her cheek. She held her breath. Don't let him be nice, she thought. Not too nice. I couldn't bear that.

'Tired?' he asked.

'Yes.'

'Was it hard work pushing the chair?'

'Not too bad, once I got used to it. You'll be getting up tomorrow?'

'Of course. They're all leaving, all except Craig. I've

asked him to stay on for a few more days. Do you mind?'

She smiled. 'Does it matter if I do?'

There was a pause. 'No. But I thought I'd ask.'

'Of course I don't mind. I like him, as a matter of fact. He's charming, he's a very strong character—and I think you've picked the right one.'

'He rather fancies you too.'

'I didn't say——' she began indignantly, and Luke laughed.

'I didn't say you *did*. And he hasn't said he fancies you. He wouldn't be so crude. But I've seen him looking at you.'

She paused, the better to choose her words. 'It's quite flattering—yes, I'd been aware of it too, but I wasn't going to say anything.' She turned to face him. 'It's nice to know someone is attracted to me—for myself.'

She felt her heartbeats quicken as his eyes subtly changed. 'Meaning?'

'Meaning nothing.' She shouldn't have said it. It had been a foolish remark, instantly regretted. She moved slightly away, and he caught her arm.

'Don't turn away from me. Look at me.'

'No.' She felt stifled.

'Damn you, *look* at me!' He forced her face round, and held it.

'All right, I will.' She stared hard at him and their eyes met in a silent clash. 'Satisfied?'

'No. I want to make love to you.'

'Do you?' Hysterical laughter bubbled up, and she

tried to suppress it, but in vain. 'You'd have a job, wouldn't you?'

He shut her up very effectively by kissing her full on the mouth, his fingers digging cruelly into her hair, making her wince, knocking all the laughter out of her in an instant. Then he pulled himself up beside her, leaned over her, pressing her back on the pillow, and kissed her again.

'Now laugh,' he said harshly, when he had done.

Sally lay back and stared wide-eyed at him, and his fingers caressed her body in a butterfly touch of exquisite gentleness, and she found herself responding instantly, treacherously.

'No, stop it——' she whispered. 'You can't—it's—imposs——'

'Nothing's impossible,' he said huskily. 'You should know me by now.'

'But—I—the nurse——'

'Lock the door,' he ordered.

'No—I——'

'*Lock* the bloody *door. Now!*'

She slid off the bed, ran over to the door, and turned the key. Then she stood there. 'I'm staying here,' she said.

He sat up. His eyes gleamed. 'I swear, if you don't come back here *now*, I'll come and get you.'

There was a heart-thudding pause. He would do it, and she dare not let him. He could hurt himself. Slowly, hesitantly, despising herself, Sally walked back to the bed and sat down on the edge.

'Now,' he said. 'Now. Just do as I tell you. But first, come nearer.' His arms were as strong—stronger perhaps—than before. Yet his touch was gentle as she lay beside him, and he began to kiss her, to touch and hold her in certain ways, and she was lost. Utterly and helplessly lost.

He was sleeping when she left him. Sister Andrews came up the corridor as Sally closed the door softly behind her. 'Mrs Vilis,' she said, and Sally put a finger to her mouth.

'Ssh! He's asleep.'

The nurse looked at her, and for a second Sally saw awareness in her eyes, instantly banished to be replaced by the cool professionalism.

'That's good. He'll be tired after all that's happened today.' She nodded briskly. She knew all right, thought Sally. 'I'll have a look in on him. He might not even need a sleeping pill, who knows?' For a moment her eyes caught Sally's and they held laughter.

'Perhaps not,' Sally smiled. 'I'll go down now and entertain my guests. Is there anything you need?'

'Nothing, thank you, Mrs Vilis. Will you be going in again to see your husband?'

'No. I'll go to bed after I've seen everyone is being looked after.'

'Then I'll say goodnight.'

'Goodnight, Sister.'

Sally ran downstairs, and Sister Andrews went into the bedroom very quietly. Then men were talking, as usual. They had adjusted to the situation, the talk was mainly about money, and all were getting on well. Cigar smoke filled the room, there was a reassuring clink of glasses, and Wilma moved discreetly among them refilling where necessary, softly spoken, completely in command. She caught Sally's eye and nodded.

'Everything okay?" Sally whispered.

'Fine, ma'am. The girls are preparing a light supper for them all.'

'Lovely. I'll just have a word with them, and then I think I'll slip off to bed. I'm very tired.'

'You do that,' said Wilma. 'You've been very busy today.'

Yes, I have, thought Sally, and she took a deep breath and went to talk to the group nearest her. Half an hour later, she was able to make her escape. All were charm itself when she spoke to them. They listened politely, they laughed at the right moments, they expressed their thanks to her for her hospitality, yet she knew, as they did, that their main concern was business, and she had no place among them. She said her goodnights and left the room, to be followed out by Craig Lamont.

'Mrs Vilis, may I have a word?'

'Of course.' She smiled at him. 'What can I do for you?'.

'Thank you for choosing me yesterday.'

'But I didn't. Luke did that. He told me to watch you—and I did, and I knew the moment to call you, that's all.'

'No, ma'am, it's not all. He relies on your judgment—but you know that already, don't you?'

She frowned. 'I'm not sure what you mean.'

'He told me—afterwards, when you left us to talk —that he needed to know your opinion—and you con-

firmed his.' He grinned down at her. 'It's wonderful
to have such a close relationship as you two have.
I didn't realise you were so newly married. May I
wish you all the happiness in the world, Mrs Vilis.
Luke is a wonderful man, but I think he deserves
you.'

It was wrong. Something was wrong. It wasn't mak-
ing sense. Sally stared at him, forced a smile, said:
'Thank you very much.' She wanted to be alone to
think. How could such a shrewd, clever man as Craig
Lamont obviously was have got things so very wrong?
'If you'll excuse me, though, I'm very tired——'

'Of course. Forgive me. I just had to let you know,
that's all. Goodnight, ma'am, and—thank you.'

'Goodnight.' She walked slowly away, aware that he
watched her go. Then the door opened, and Craig
went back into the dining room. She went up the stairs,
and her legs felt very heavy. She suddenly felt exhausted, as though she had been running for a long
time.

The next day, Sally felt depressed. She tried to throw
it off, she acted the part of hostess capably, talked to
the guests, supervised Luke's being taken downstairs
to meet his colleagues, and smiled, and generally took
care of everything. Yet the grey sad feeling would not
go away. Nine days to go, that was all. It would soon
pass. She had no appetite, and ate as little as politely
possible without causing comment. But one person
noticed—Wilma, who missed nothing.

After a late lunch the men departed for their planes,
and the house became quieter. Only Craig was left,

and he and Luke sat by the pool discussing all they had to discuss, while Sally went up to her room to lie down. Wilma came up, knocked, and went in.

'Oh, Wilma, what is it? Any problems?' Sally sat up in bed.

'No, ma'am, everything's fine. 'Cept I was concerned about you.'

'Me?' Her astonishment showed. 'Why?'

'Oh, ma'am, you ate hardly anything at breakfast and lunch. And you—forgive me, it's not my place to speak, and you can tell me off right now if you wish—you have a sadness about you I can't explain. I only want you to be happy. Am I doing anything wrong? Just tell me.'

'No. You're marvellous.' Sally stopped. 'I am a little depressed today, perhaps it's tiredness—yet you've done all the work.' She managed an impish grin. 'It's just one of those things, really. I'll be better later on.'

'You sure now?'

Sally put her hands to her face and burst into tears. 'I don't know,' she sobbed.

'Ah, there now, tell Wilma. Why, honey, I knew there was something amiss. You can tell me.' The older woman put her arms round Sally.

'I can't. I can't tell anyone.' Her voice was muffled with sobs.

'You can. But don't try. Just remember, I'm always here to listen. Is it something to do with Mister Luke?'

'Yes. But—don't you see—I can't tell you. You love him like a son, and that's as it should be. I've only just arrived—I'm nothing to you—oh, Wilma, I'm not making sense, I know—it's best we forget about all this. I'll be all right soon. I'll pull myself together, don't worry.'

'You need some help,' said Wilma worriedly. 'I can't leave you like this. It wouldn't be right. Shall I get the nurse to see you?'

'There's nothing she can do. There's nothing medically wrong with me, I'm sure of that. It's here that's the problem,' and she touched her heart. 'There's no pill to cure a broken heart, is there?' She hadn't meant to say it, but the words had come out of their own volition.

'Oh, my lord, what is it?' gasped Wilma.

'Don't you know? Can't you guess? I love Luke, but he doesn't love me—and I'm not sure if I can stand it much longer.'

Wilma's eyes filled with tears. 'Honey, you'd better tell me everything,' she said softly.

Sally looked at her. 'All right, I will.' And so, softly at first, she began to tell the housekeeper all that had happened, right from the very beginning. She spared nothing. She didn't spare herself. The truth came out, and as she told the sympathetic woman her heart lifted slightly for the telling of it. When she had finished, she waited for she knew not what.

There was a long silence, then Wilma spoke: 'Now I understand. Ah, but I'm glad you told me. What a sad, mixed-up world it is!'

'So you see why I've got to leave him?' Sally's eyes held a desperate appeal.

'But he's learnin' to love you. I can see it——'

'No! You mustn't say that! Don't you *see*—it's Laura that he loves, Laura that he thinks of all the time. I can't live in her shadow, Wilma, I can't!'

'Are you *sure*, honey?'

'Yes, I know. Oh, Wilma, I'm sorry. I shouldn't have told you—but I feel a bit better now. I'm only sorry I've burdened you. You're so kind, you're so very good . . .'

'Ah, hush now. I'm just me.' Wilma took Sally's hands and clasped them firmly. 'T'ain't no burden for me, just remember that. I can take it—and if the telling's helped you, then that's all that counts. Rest now, I'll bring you a cool drink later. I respect you, Mrs Vilis, and whatever you do is fine by me. But don't rush off—think first. Promise me that.'

'I promise.' Sally lay back. 'I promise—I'll try.'

'Then sleep now, and rest yourself. I'll be back later.' Wilma went silently out. Sally heaved a huge sigh, and closed her eyes. Wilma had understood. She had understood everything, and neither condoned nor condemned. She was a far wiser woman than Sally had even imagined. After a while she slept. And she dreamed of Laura.

The days passed, and everything on the surface was normal. Luke grew gradually stronger, and had a pair of crutches brought so that he could walk—after a fashion—clumsily and awkwardly at first, but gradually with greater skill. Craig Lamont left three days later, and then they were alone—save for Sister Andrews, the younger nurse, Andrea, and occasional visits from Doctor Rossi, who had solemnly presented

Luke with a bottle of champagne which they had then drunk.

Wilma was her usual busy efficient self, but her concern was for Sally, and it showed. Luke remarked on it at dinner one night. It was the eighth day. Sally laughed. 'We got on well, that's all.'

'I'm glad to see it. She fusses over you like a mother hen.'

'Does she? Then I like being fussed. More salad, Luke?'

It was easier when she kept calm. Her resolve wouldn't waver this way. Luke gave her an odd look, but said nothing. That night he made love to her fiercely, and she responded, yet at the same time keeping a part of her heart aloof. It mustn't matter, it didn't have to matter she told herself. It was purely physical on both sides, and if he thought of Laura it must not hurt her any longer, for in three days she was leaving him—for ever.

She visited Rosa and Alistair, got the London address from them, and put it in her bag. Only then she made the mistake of leaving her bag in the bedroom.

The evening after, she went up to the bedroom to say goodnight to Luke, and he was holding her handbag. At first she didn't realise, then, as he spoke, his voice deceptively soft, awareness swept over her.

'What's this?' he asked, holding up the sheet of paper.

She snatched it from him. 'What are you doing in my handbag?' Her cheeks were flushed, a pulse beat rapidly in her throat, and she fought rising panic.

'You left it here and it fell on the floor and opened. I reached down to put everything back and this fell out.' He stared at the paper she now held. 'Mr and Mrs A. Herrick, care of Mrs Farrier, 27 Queens——'

'All right, I can read too,' Sally interrupted. She put it in her handbag and closed it.

'It's in Rosa's writing——' he began.

'How do you know that?' she demanded.

'She bought us a present, remember? It's quite distinctive. Now what would they be going to London for—or rather, why haven't you mentioned it?'

'I forgot.'

'Oh, come on now,' his eyes narrowed, 'don't take me for a fool. My God, do I *look* stupid?'

'No. I'm not going to discuss it, it's quite unimportant. They're going for a holiday and I'm going to write to them.'

'You liar!'

Her eyes blazed. 'So I'm a liar? Good! There's nothing further to say. Goodnight.'

'Sit down,' ordered Luke. 'I've not finished yet.'

'Well, I have. I'm ...'

'Sit down, or by God I'll pull you down!'

Sally sat at the furthest edge of the bed, and waited. He looked at her. 'Now,' he said, 'tell me why they're going.'

'Uncle Alistair is ill. They're going to see a specialist.' She hadn't broken her promise to Rosa.

'How ill?'

'Very ill.'

'Did you know this when you agreed to marry me?'

She looked directly into his eyes. 'Yes, I did.'

Strength filled her. He couldn't stop them going, she would see to that, even if it meant cutting all the phones. She was quite determined on that point. 'It's very funny, really. I did something quite unselfish—for me; even you should see the amusing side to that.'

He ignored the sarcasm. 'So that was why you agreed so readily? Because of your uncle?'

She spoke very slowly. 'What other reason could there have possibly been? Did you think I loved you?' She began to laugh.

He reached over and pulled her towards him. Roughly he shook her. 'Stop laughing!'

'I can't—I can't——' It was threatening to turn to hysteria. She felt herself going breathless. The next moment his hand stung her cheek, she gasped, filled with shock, and stopped laughing. She stood up, her bosom heaving.

'That does it,' she said quietly. 'I'm going to my room.'

'Wait—Sally——' But she had gone. She closed the door behind her with finality. She would not go in there again, not while he was there. It was a simple decision to make. And in the morning she would get John to take her to the airstrip and see about a plane home—to England.


Rosa and Alistair were safely away, and on the following morning Sally was going to leave Vilis House with the minimum of luggage, and make her own departure. She was no longer calm—if indeed she ever had been. She was nervous, with no appetite, and near to tears all the time. Luke's mood was aggressive, unapproachable, edgy. It must have been obvious to the entire household, and Wilma was clearly unhappy. She and Sally spoke quietly on that last evening, safely in the kitchen, drinking iced tea while Sally traced endless meaningless patterns on the table with her finger.

'But can't you see,' Sally burst out, after a final attempt on Wilma's part to make her stay, 'it's impossible? He won't get better while I'm here, that's obvious. You've seen what he's like. He's had Sister Andrews nearly in tears—and I would have thought that impossible—and the young nurse, Andrea, is a nervous wreck.' She put her hand to her burning forehead. 'It's me. I know it's me. The sooner I've gone the sooner he'll get over it.'

'Will he?' asked Wilma.

'What do you mean?'

'He could get worse.'

'No, Wilma. You know the truth of it all. He's regretting this bizarre marriage. I'll be doing him a good turn. I'll write him a letter telling him so tonight.' She touched the other's hand. 'You're so good. I'm sorry it's ending like this. But there's no other way.' She stood up. 'I'm going to have a bath and an early night. I'll see you in the morning.'

'Sleep well,' said Wilma.

'I'll try.'

Sally crept up the stairs, and into her own room, the one she had slept in since her own collapse. There she packed a case, then sat down and wrote a letter to Luke. It was the hardest letter she had ever written in her life. She left the envelope unsealed, because in the morning her last act would be to return his wedding ring. Then, letter completed, she went to have a bath.

She slept badly that night, and woke at dawn relieved that the night was over. She went out and walked round the garden for the last time, and her heart was filled with pain. Yet there was no going back. It was all over. Gradually, as she walked round in the coolness of the morning, she knew that she was doing the right thing. She would get over it in a while, she knew that. She was young, and strong—and a different person from the one who had arrived on Adelana only weeks previously. She had told Luke that in the letter. She had told him that she had learned a lot, and his plan, in that sense, had worked. Whether he would care or not was a different matter.

She went into the house, into the kitchen to see Wilma and to drink her first cup of coffee of the day. All too soon she would be gone.

Sally saw the lights of Heathrow in the distance. Back home from holiday, she thought, and there was a bitter taste in her mouth. A couple of nights at her flat, perhaps a meeting with Rosa and Uncle Alistair, and then she was going to drive up north to a cottage her mother owned in the Lake District. Her mother never went any more, and Sally had a key. And there she would stay for as long as she needed to recover from whatever ailed her. Then she would decide her future. It would all work out in the end.

She heard the instructions, and fastened her seat belt as the plane began its descent. Soon she would be home. Soon . . .

Tears filled her eyes. Goodbye, Luke, she thought. In spite of everything, you have succeeded in your plan. She turned her head to see the runway whizzing past, then a slowing, a stopping, a final braking, and the plane stopped. It was all over.

# CHAPTER ELEVEN

SALLY drove up the M6 towards Kendal, rain lashing the car, and she longed for the warmth and quiet of the cottage she had always loved. To go there was like going home. It had often served as a bolthole with one or two friends when the pace of London life grew too hectic, and now it would provide her with the peaceful atmosphere she needed. On the back seat, together with all her provisions, was a stack of books, and a portable radio. She had never liked being alone, but now she longed to be so. In that too, she had changed.

She arrived as it was growing dusk, took all her things in, locked the car, and walked across a field to the neighbouring farm to let them know of her arrival, and order milk and eggs. The farmer's wife, Mrs Murray, welcomed her, and invited her in for a cup of tea. A plump, motherly soul, she never asked questions, merely accepted the comings and goings of those strange London people, and promised Sally all the milk, eggs and cheese she needed.

Sally set off back across the field, clutching the pint of milk to her, feet squelching on the softened ground, and breathed deeply of the cool evening air. She had promised to keep in touch with Rosa and Alistair when she had seen them the previous day, and she intended to telephone as often as she could. There was no phone at the cottage, but there was a public call-box half a mile down the road.

She opened the door and went in, made herself a cup of coffee and a sandwich and went straight to bed. And there she slept until midday the following day, the sleep of utter exhaustion.

She began to get herself organised. Only thus was she able to put Luke out of her mind. She would go for long rides in the car, do her shopping in Kendal, a mere five miles away, and spend her evenings reading, with the radio as background. Then early to bed and early to rise. And it worked, after a fashion. She regained her appetite, she walked for miles, and the high spot of her day was the evening phone call to Rosa and Alistair.

When she had been there for two weeks she got up one morning, ate her toast, drank her tea, and promptly brought it all up again. She stood by the sink in the kitchen, dazed, knowing at last something she had suspected for a week but put out of her mind. Then, very carefully, she went to fetch her diary out of her handbag, sat down, opened it, and began to calculate.

It was just after nine. Sally put on her coat, went out, got into her car and drove to the telephone down the road.

'Rosa? It's me, Sally.'

'Sally! It's morning—this'll cost you a packet. What is it?'

'Oh God, I've got to tell somebody. I think I'm pregnant.'

She heard Rosa's indrawn breath at the other end of the line. 'Oh, Sally—do you want me to come up?'

She clutched eagerly at the straw. 'Can you? Oh no, you can't leave Uncle Alistair——'

'Listen, he's had lots of tests, and we're just waiting now, and he's resting for a few days. Of course I will.' Sally pressed in another tenpence as the pips went, and heard Rosa continue: 'Listen, I'll get things moving this end, check with the specialist and so on. Ring me back in half an hour. Can you do that?'

'Can I? Of course I can. Half an hour.' She said goodbye and hung up, feeling better than she had for weeks. Rosa would come, and she desperately needed someone to talk to—oh, how she needed someone!

She drove to Kendal to buy food, found a telephone kiosk, and dialled the London number again. The fingers she had kept crossed since the previous call had obviously done the trick. Rosa was going to come, and would want meeting at Kendal station. She gave Sally the time, and Sally promised to be there, then went home to prepare another bed.

'What are you going to do? Have you decided?' Rosa sat in the comfortable lounge and looked across at Sally.

'Do you mean—abortion?'

'Yes.'

Sally shook her head. 'I couldn't. That's all there is to it. I know it's fashionable, but not for me. And—in a strange way—I want this baby. It's all I'll have of Luke. Do you understand?'

Rosa smiled. 'Oh yes, I understand. But I had to ask, to know.'

'Of course you did.'

'Then what will you do? You can't stay up here alone, love. You must move back to London, you must see that.'

'Yes. I've thought about it quite a bit since phoning you this morning. I'll go back, eventually. Perhaps in a week or two.'

'Sally,' Rosa began very quietly, 'you wouldn't consider . . .' she hesitated.

Sally's heart began to thud. 'What?'

'Telling Luke.'

'No. Never!' She shook her head violently. 'He'd think I was after money, and I'm not. I won't ever touch a penny of his.'

'But you are his wife.'

'Legally—yes. And we both know what a farce it is. No, Rosa, that's out. Do you think he'd care anyway?'

'You want an honest answer?' Rosa looked directly at her.

'Yes, I do.'

'You think you know him better than I do?'

Sally laughed. 'I know him very well. Promise me you'll never tell him?'

'Of course I promise,' Rosa looked shocked. 'Your life's your own. It's up to you to make the decisions. But——' she shrugged, 'I just thought—that's all.'

'I know. I'm glad you could come up, truly I am. It's like having a sister to confide in.'

'That's the nicest thing you could ever say.' Rosa smiled gently. 'I do like you, Sally. I'm sorry I didn't at first——'

'It's all right,' said Sally. 'I didn't particularly like myself then. I've changed, I know that. I hope we'll always be friends—as well as aunt and niece, of course.' At which they both laughed, so much that they didn't hear the knocking at the door at first, until it came louder. They looked at each other in alarm.

'Who——' began Rosa.

'I don't know. Perhaps Mrs Murray. I'll go and see.' Sally got up, went into the hall and opened the door.

Luke was standing there, supported by John on one side, and a crutch at the other. For a wordless moment Sally just stared, then he said:

'Aren't you going to ask me in? I've come a hell of a long way, and my legs won't hold me much longer.'

'Luke!'

'You did recognise me then? Good. Please may we come in?'

She stood back, looked round to see Rosa gaping at them from the living room door, and said faintly: 'Yes. Come in.'

It was Rosa who made the coffee, saw Luke into a comfortable chair, with John's assistance, Rosa who took charge. Sally could hardly speak, let alone move. She heard them talking around her, but she didn't take it in. It wasn't until the door closed that she realised Luke and she were alone.

'They've gone,' he said gently. 'We booked two rooms at an hotel in Kendal. John's gone there with Rosa. She can have my room. Because we're going to talk, you and I.'

Sally looked at him. 'Talk?'

'Yes, talk. Like why did you leave me?'

She shook her head. She couldn't believe he was really there.

'Sally, please come over here.' He said it very gently, and she obediently went over and sat beside him.

'Sally, I love you. I love you very much.'

'No, you don't.' She felt as if she was discussing someone else. 'You love Laura. It's all right, I'm used to it.'

'I love you,' he said again. 'You are my present and my future, the woman I want to be with for the rest of my life. I love Laura, and always will, but only as someone I once loved when I was young. Do you understand that?'

'No. It was her you thought of when we—when we——'

'Oh God!' He held her hand. 'Only once, at first—and then—you. You only. I didn't even realise what was happening to me until it was too late.' He sighed. 'It was Wilma who gave me the biggest telling off of my life.'

'Wilma?' she giggled.

'Yes.'

'She told *you* off?'

'Yes. And how! I was like a bear with a sore head before you left—I was, apparently, according to her, even worse after you'd gone. I was frantic. I couldn't move with that damned plaster on my leg. All I could do was rage. Then she gave me her notice—and told me why. She didn't mince her words, she gave it me straight. I asked her, if I brought you back, whether she'd reconsider her notice.' He looked at Sally. 'Then she smiled, and that said it all. So I came.'

'I love you,' she said gently.

'Do you? She told me you did, but I was past believing anything.'

'Oh yes, I love you. But I thought—all the time—it was Laura, and that hurt too much.'

'There will always be a certain place for Laura, but you must understand, just a sweet memory of a dear love. I never thought I would love any woman again. Then you came into my life, and gradually, I knew, and I thought it couldn't happen again, but it has. The love I feel for you fills my whole world. I will be nothing without you now, Sally, nothing. Am I making you understand?'

She sighed gently and took his hand. 'I think so. Luke, there's something I must tell you. It's the reason I had Rosa here.'

'What is it?' he asked.

'Can you guess?'

He looked at her. He stared deep into her eyes, and she willed him to know, and saw a dawning knowledge in his. 'Sally, don't keep me guessing. Is it—what I think?'

'I'm having a baby.'

He leaned forward, and for a moment she thought it was with shock, as he closed his eyes. Then he opened them, and she saw the love shining out, filling her, surrounding her, and she caught her breath.

'Oh, my darling, my dearest—I'd pick you up and dance round the room with you if I could! And did you *know* when you left me?'

'No. I'm not positive now—not officially, that is—but yes, I knew this morning.'

'This is wonderful! You must take care of yourself. We must go to a doctor's in the morning. We might have to stay here for a while until it's okay for you to fly back to Adelana ...' Sally left him and walked quietly across the room to drawn the curtains.

'I'll make you a drink,' she said. 'We can make our plans when we go to bed. You must be tired—and you do need looking after.'

'Not for long. See?' He struggled to his feet, nearly overbalancing, held the crutch, and walked towards her. 'I'll soon have both my legs again—and I'll take care of you.' He looked down at her as she put her arms round him. 'I'll take of you for always.'

'Always?' she teased.

'Mmm, yes.' He kissed her tenderly. 'Never mind the drink. Let's go to bed. I want to hold you, and tell you all my plans.'

'You're bossing me!' she scolded.

'Yes, I suppose I am. Can you learn to live with a bossy man?'

'I'll have to think about it.' She laughed, and hugged him. 'I've thought about it, and I can't imagine anything more wonderful.' They walked slowly towards the door, and she switched off the light. Then, going very carefully, Luke occasionally stumbling, swearing, and then laughing, they went up the stairs to bed. Their life together had truly begun.

# Harlequin
## Announces the
# COLLECTION EDITIONS
## OF 1978

Harlequin's Collection 12

ANDREA BLAKE
**Night of the Hurrica**

Harlequin's Collection 106     1.25

ANNE WEALE
**If This Is Love**

stories of special
beauty and significance

# 25 Beautiful stories of particular merit

In 1976 we introduced the first 100 Harlequin Collections — a selection of titles chosen from our best sellers of the past 20 years. This series, a trip down memory lane, proved how great romantic fiction can be timeless and appealing from generation to generation. Perhaps because the theme of love and romance is eternal, and, when placed in the hands of talented, creative, authors whose true gift lies in their ability to write from the heart, the stories reach a special level of brilliance that the passage of time cannot dim. Like a treasured heirloom, an antique of superb craftsmanship, a beautiful gift from someone loved, — these stories too, have a special significance that transcends the ordinary.

# Here's your 1978 Harlequin Collection Editions . . .

More great Harlequin 1978 Collection Editions . . .

**122 Moon Over Africa**
Pamela Kent
(#983)

**123 Island In The Dawn**
Averil Ives
(#984)

**124 Lady In Harley Street**
Anne Vinton
(#985)

**125 Play The Tune Softly**
Amanda Doyle
(#1116)

**126 Will You Surrender?**
Joyce Dingwell
(#1179)

**Original Harlequin Romance numbers in brackets**

---

# ORDER FORM—Harlequin Reader Service

In U.S.A.:
MPO Box 707,
Niagara Falls, N.Y. 14302

In Canada:
649 Ontario St., Stratford,
Ontario N5A 6W2

Please send me the following Harlequin Collection novels. I am enclosing my check or money order for $1.25 for each novel ordered, plus 25¢ to cover postage and handling.

| ☐ 102 | ☐ 107 | ☐ 112 | ☐ 117 | ☐ 122 |
| ☐ 103 | ☐ 108 | ☐ 113 | ☐ 118 | ☐ 123 |
| ☐ 104 | ☐ 109 | ☐ 114 | ☐ 119 | ☐ 124 |
| ☐ 105 | ☐ 110 | ☐ 115 | ☐ 120 | ☐ 125 |
| ☐ 106 | ☐ 111 | ☐ 116 | ☐ 121 | ☐ 126 |

Number of novels checked _____ @ $1.25 each = $ _____

N.Y. and N.J. residents add appropriate sales tax   $ _____

Postage and handling                                $ ___.25

                                         TOTAL   $ _____

NAME _____
(Please print)
ADDRESS _____

CITY _____

STATE/PROV. _____ ZIP/POSTAL CODE _____

ROM 2177

Offer expires December 31, 1978

# Poignant tales of love, conflict, romance and adventure

*Harlequin Presents...*

Elegant and sophisticated novels of
**great romantic fiction . . .**
12 All time best sellers.

Join the millions of avid Harlequin readers all over the world who delight in the magic of a really exciting novel.

**From the library of Harlequin Presents all time best sellers — we are proud and pleased to make available the 12 selections listed here.**

Combining all the essential elements you expect of great story telling, and bringing together your very favourite authors — you'll thrill to these exciting tales of love, conflict, romance, sophistication and adventure. You become involved with characters who are interesting, vibrant, and alive. Their individual conflicts, struggles, needs, and desires, grip you, the reader, until the final page.

# Complete and mail this coupon today!

# ORDER FORM

**Harlequin Reader Service**

In U.S.A.:
MPO Box 707,
Niagara Falls, N.Y. 14302

In Canada:
649 Ontario St., Stratford,
Ontario N5A 6W2

Please send me the following Harlequin Presents . . . I am
enclosing my check or money order for $1.25 for each
novel ordered, plus 25¢ to cover postage and handling.

☐ 75 Dare I Be Happy

☐ 76 Heart of the Lion

☐ 77 The Japanese Screen

☐ 78 A Man Like Daintree

☐ 79 The Black Eagle

☐ 80 Innocent Deception

☐ 81 The Iron Man

☐ 82 Copper Moon

☐ 83 Yet Love Remains

☐ 84 That Summer Of
Surrender

☐ 85 Love in Disguise

☐ 86 Rachel Trevellyan

Number of novels checked \_\_\_\_\_ @ $1.25 each = $ _____

N.Y. and N.J. residents add appropriate sales tax $ _____

Postage and handling $ \_\_\_.25

TOTAL $ _____

NAME _____
(Please Print)

ADDRESS _____

CITY _____

STATE / PROV. _____ ZIP / POSTAL CODE

ROM 2177

Offer expires December 31, 1978